Beast: New Chapter

Previously titled

Beasts: New Beginnings

By: Natavia

Kanye
Twenty years later...

The sound of my alarm woke me up. I knocked it off of my nightstand as a growl slipped from my lips because I hated to wake up in the morning. I enjoyed my nights and would rather sleep all day. I took a shower then got dressed for school. I didn't understand why Akea, my twin brother, and I had to go to college. We had all of our lives to go to college. I walked out of my bedroom and headed down the stairs. We lived in an estate far away from the city. The closest home to us was twenty minutes away. We needed the big house because seventeen people occupied it. The home had twenty bedrooms and only twelve were filled— the pack was big, so I knew they'd be filling up quickly.

I walked into the gym room; my father and his brother, Izra, were lifting weights. My father, who the pack called "Goon", sat the weight down and looked at me. "Partied hard on a school night?" he asked.

Izra walked passed me and patted my back. "Next time hide the liquor bottle," he whispered before he walked out of the room.

"College isn't for me. Maybe for Akea, but not for me. Why can't I just work in the family business? I'm a werewolf that lives for eternity. What purpose does college serve?" I asked my father and he growled at me. His eyes turned blue when he stood up.

"College will give you knowledge. Do you want to be a dumb immortal? That knowledge will stick with you and you can pass it down to your pups in the future. We need to learn about what's in the world that we live in," he said to me. Akea walked down the hall dressed in a button-up shirt, khakis, and a tie.

"I guess Akea blends in well with the science geeks," I said out loud.

"Akea is on the Dean's List," our father spat.

"Did you forget your pocket protector?" I asked Akea. My father slapped me on the back of my head.

"Leave him alone, Kanye, and I mean it," he said. Monifa walked passed me with her nose frowned up.

"Good morning uncle Goon," Monifa said before she kissed his cheek. She kissed Akea's cheek and looked at me.

"Where is my kiss?" I asked her.

"Wherever your common sense is at. What did you do to my necklace? I know you came into my room because I could smell your scent. You better get to talkin', Kanye, or else," she said.

"Or else what? I wasn't in your funky room," I said to her and she mushed me. Akea and my father laughed as they walked away.

I mushed her back and she growled at me, "I'm going to kick your arrogant ass if you step foot in my room again. Don't touch my shit," she said to me.

"With your ugly self," I said to her and she pushed me. I pushed her back. "Don't mess with me this morning, Monifa, and I mean it," I said to her.

"Where is my neckless that Yardi gave to me?" she asked me.

"I don't know. Ask his punk-ass where it's at. You shouldn't be messing around with a human anyway," I spat.

"Don't you mess with human females?" she asked me.

"None of your business," I said before I walked out of her face.

"I can't stand you, Kanye!" she screamed at me.

"I can't stand your ass, neither!" I shouted back at her.

"Watch your mouth!" my mother yelled at me when she walked down the stairs and I kissed her cheek.

"Good morning, Ma. How are you feeling? You look beautiful," I said to her. Her frown turned into a slight smile as her mood softened.

"Good morning, handsome. Did you have fun last night?" she asked.

"It was aight," I said. I had a threesome for the first time with two college chicks and it wasn't as fun as I thought it would be. They cried every time I entered them and eventually I went limp. I was completely turned off but it was something about human women that I was attracted to.

"You need to take college a bit more seriously. You are a very smart boy but you are just too stubborn to learn," she said.

"I will, Ma, and see you later," I said. I walked out of the door and got into my black sports car with the drop top. I revved the engine.

"So, you were just going to leave me, huh?" Zaan asked me.

"I thought you had a hangover," I said to him and he got inside my car.

"I did until my father came in my room with some type of drink. Nigga, when I sipped on that drink, it made me feel like a new wolf," he said.

"Uncle Elle always got something special," I said. The twins Baneet and Chancy walked out of the house, laughing and giggling.

"Baneet got some juicy legs. Juicer than a raw T-bone steak," Zaan said as he lustfully stared at her.

"Dayo is going to mess you up," I said.

"I will take one for the team. Look at her ass and hips," Zaan said.

"Come here, Baneet!" Zaan called out to her.

"I'm running late for school! Call me," Baneet yelled out before she got into her truck.

"You got it bad, bro," I said to Zaan.

"I can't help it. She is beautiful and her smooth, dark chocolate skin is like silk," Zaan said.

"Dayo is going to bite your head off," I said to him and he waved me off.
"Are you riding to school with us?" I called out to Akea when he walked out of the house.

"No, go ahead," he replied.

Akea and I wasn't close because he always avoided being around me. I picked on him at times because that was the only way I could communicate with him. In school, he'd walked passed me like he didn't know me. He even talked to Zaan more than he talked to me.

"Harry Potter-looking muthafucka," I mumbled as I pulled off.
"What did you do to Monifa's necklace? I heard you two arguing," Zaan said to me.

"I'm going to take it to Beastly Treasures and get real diamonds put inside of it. I can't believe her punk-ass boyfriend got her fake diamonds. I hope she ain't screwing him, neither," I told Zaan.

"What if she is?" he asked me and I growled. I gritted my teeth as I clutched the steering wheel. "She knows better," I replied.

"Y'all don't even get along. Why not tell her you feel some type of way about her?" he asked.

"Because I don't. I just don't want her messing with someone who doesn't appreciate her enough to give her real diamonds. Even if he can't afford it, he should've waited or got her something else," I said and Zaan shook his head.

"Bro, you got it bad for her, just admit it. I think she has it bad for you, too. Y'all niggas are in love," Zaan joked.

"Yeah, right. You are a fool if you think I will fall in love," I spat.

"You was in love with Arya," he said. Arya was Dayo's and Anik's oldest daughter. She wasn't their blood daughter but Anik raised her since she was a pup.

"I was young and I wouldn't call that love. It was more like lust because all I wanted to do was bang her one good time," I said and he chuckled.

****

After my third class, I ran into Monifa. She was coming out of the bathroom by the cafeteria. She was texting on her cell phone when she bumped into me.

"Damn it, idiot! Watch where you are going!" she said to me.

"Who are you talking to like that?" I asked. My eyes gazed down her neckline and landed on her ample breasts. She wore a shirt that showed enough cleavage. She closed her shirt up and crossed her arms.

"You can't hide those big jugs," I teased. She tried to walk away but I grabbed her hand. Monifa was gorgeous and she knew it. Her skin was the color of peanut butter and her eyes slanted into the shape of almonds. Her lips were full, and besides her beauty, I couldn't help but to stare at her wide hips.

"Why do you always got to be mean?" I asked her.

"I heard about your night in class today. You had a threesome?" she asked with sarcasm in her voice.

"Why does it matter?" I replied.

"It doesn't, creep," she said and snatched away from me.

"What did I do to you?" I asked and she walked away from me. Her boyfriend, Yardi, walked over to her and put his arm around her shoulder. He kissed her lips and she didn't pull back. His hand squeezed her round bottom and he whispered in her ear. I wanted to bite his head off. It wasn't school that really bothered me. I didn't like that Monifa went to the same school and I had to see males flop all over her. It made my blood boil. The beast in me wanted to kill Yardi. Male wolves were possessive and territorial. I gave him the head nod when he looked at me and smirked. He knew how to make my blood boil by using Monifa.

I'm going to kill your lame ass one day, I thought to myself.

Monifa

I walked through the mall with Baneet and Chancy. The three of us were very close.

We entered an Urban fashion store. There was a big college party on campus after the football game that night.

"Damn it, do they believe in size fourteen's around here?" I asked out loud.

"Right. Only one who can fit this crap is Chancy," Baneet said. Chancy was slim and curvaceous while Baneet and I were a little heavier. We possessed wide hips, thick thighs, and big butts.

"And I'm not even interested in none of this," Chancy said as she popped her gum.

"We should get an apartment away from home," Baneet said.
"Our parents are very old-fashioned. The pack must live together and blah, blah, blah," I said.

"I like it home," Chancy said.

"You just like being around Akea," I said and Baneet laughed.

"Akea doesn't pay nobody any mind," Baneet replied as she looked through the rack.

"If I had a brother like Kanye I would be mad at the world, too. Kanye is an arrogant asshole and he makes my skin crawl. He is nothing but a chick magnet," I said.

"Speak of the devil," Chancy said. When I turned around, Kanye and Zaan walked into the store and I must admit that Kanye was borderline gorgeous. Kanye had to be around six-foot-two and had a very nice build; his skin was the color of copper. His arms and chest were solid which gave him extra sex appeal. He had markings all over his body that he inherited from his roots. We all had a few but Kanye's tribal markings were different, like his father. He wore a sleeveless shirt and a pair of shorts and tennis shoes. His hair was tapered on the sides and the middle was wavy. Everything on him was perfect. Zaan was very attractive also; he was more of a lean build and taller than Kanye. Zaan had pretty, dark skin and he wore his hair in locks like his father, Elle, used to before he cut them off.

Kanye's eyes turned ice blue when he saw me. I rolled my eyes at him. "Why can't I get away from him?" I asked out loud.

"Because you want some of him," Baneet teased me. Zaan kissed Baneet on her cheek and she blushed. Everyone knew they were low-key dating, all except for her father, Dayo.

"I got enough of you this morning and now this?" I asked Kanye.

"Shut up. I just came in here to get something to wear for tonight," he said and walked passed me. I stared at the tribal markings that wrapped around his muscled arm and neck. When he looked at me, I hurriedly turn my head.

"You know you can't fit shit up in here, Monifa," Kanye said to me and laughed. Chancy and Baneet giggled and I growled at them. I stormed out of the store with Chancy following behind me.

"He makes me sick," I said out loud. A group of cute guys walked passed us. Chancy waved at them—she was a flirt.

"What are you two getting into?" one of them asked us. He wasn't something special to look at. Kanye, Baneet, and Zaan walked out of the store. Kanye had a bag in his hand. When he saw the group of guys, his facial expression changed—he was pissed off. He stood next to me.

"What y'all niggas want?" Kanye asked the guys and put his arm around me. His voice and appearance was intimidating because he looked and acted like a "thug". When the group of guys walked off, he unwrapped his arm from around me.

"I'll see you at home, hot ass," he said to me before he walked off. Zaan kissed Baneet's lips and smirked at me before he left out of the mall with Kanye. For some reason Zaan thought that me and Kanye was in love.

"Why am I turned on?" I asked them then faked a gag.

"You two need to stop it. Izra will get over it eventually. Adika is mad cool and I don't think she will trip over it," Chancy said.

"Stop what?" I asked.

"Y'all two are in love. He is jealous over you and you are jealous over him. When he comes around, you blush and you can't fake it anymore. That being mean and acting annoyed role is getting played out, sista. Y'all two are in love," Chancy said.

"I will throw up if you say that shit again. I'm head over heels in love with Yardi," I said and Chancy rolled her eyes.

"Girl, please. That guy is whack and his game is lame. That whole jock attitude is soooooo back in the day. Besides, you know a werewolf pleasure is off the scale. When a male werewolf bites, it's like no other. I heard it gives you an orgasmic high and it makes you cum so hard that it'll stop your heart," Chancy said. The thought of Kanye biting me to mark me caused butterflies to form in my stomach.

******

A few hours later...

The hot water wasn't working inside of my room so I headed to the hall bathroom. I pushed the door open and jumped when I saw Kanye peeing in the toilet. My eyes darted to his dick and he just stood there unbothered that I invaded his privacy. He sniffed the air and growled while he stared at me.

"Are you aroused?" he asked me.

"You jerk!" I said then hurried out of the bathroom. I went inside of my room and locked the door. I fanned myself to cool off because my body temperature was overheating. I settled for the cold water because I needed a cold shower to cool off. Visions of Kanye touching me filled my head and a strong ache formed between my legs. His scent even drove me crazy because it was still in my room from when he took my necklace. He denied it but I knew for a fact he did it because his scent was strong and it lingered. After I got dressed, I headed out with Baneet and Chancy.

Arya was getting out of her car when we walked out of the house.

"Look at you three all dolled up. Where are y'all going and did your fathers see you all leave out? Y'all clothes are squeezing everything," she said and laughed.

"No, they didn't see us, that's why we are trying to hurry up and leave. We are grown anyway," Chancy said.

"Our father doesn't seem to think that," Arya said to her sisters and yawned.

"I'm tired. I had a long day at the warehouse," she said. Arya helped out with Ula's and Amadi's skincare products.

"We will see you later. Don't wait up," Chancy said to her before she went into the house. Arya kept it cordial with me because we were in the same pack, but I felt like she didn't like me. When I was younger, she was like a big sister to me but after a while, she kind of started ignoring me.

"Chancy, it's your turn to drive. We've been in my truck almost all day," Baneet said and Chancy sucked her teeth.

"Fine!" she said and we headed to her car. Yardi sent me a message telling me that him and his frat buddies were already at the party.

"We are having fun tonight!" I shouted.

"I know I am," Chancy said.

"Hot ass," Baneet teased.

****

An hour later...

"Where is that necklace I bought for you?" Yardi asked me.

"It's home," I lied. He pulled me into him then kissed my lips. I wrapped my arms around his neck and kissed him back. I pulled away from him after a while and sipped my spiked punch. The party was crowded. Baneet and Chancy stayed on the dancefloor. Chancy was really into the party as she danced seductively. I pulled Yardi into me and grinded on him. His arms wrapped around my hips. Yardi was handsome. He stood at six-feet and had a football player build to him. We dated since my freshman year of college which was two years prior. I was his tutor then one thing led to another.

Kanye walked through the crowd with Zaan. The girls rushed to Kanye like he was a celebrity. I made all of them fall on top of each other and the ceiling light blew out. I'm a witch and werewolf. I liked my beast, but my witch was what I loved even more. My mother taught me a lot of spells and I had been practicing them with her since I could remember. Kanye looked at me because he knew I was the cause of it. I gave him the finger and he smiled at me. He blew me a kiss then winked at me and I forgot all about Yardi and what he was talking about.

"Do you hear me?" Yardi asked.

"What?" I asked him.

"Are you coming back to my room with me?" he asked me.

"I'm spending a spa day with my mom and my cousins, tomorrow. It's an all-girls outing," I lied.

"When are you going to make time for me?" Yardi asked me.

"Next weekend, I'm all yours," I replied. Kanye looked at me then looked at Yardi while a female stood in his face, wanting his attention. Kanye ignored her but she turned his head so that he could face her. Her name was Jaysha and word around campus was that he was messing around with her. She was a human and was very popular on campus. Her parents were wealthy and she was quick to throw it out there that she was rich. Rumor was that before she met Kanye, she got a boy locked up because he dumped her. I hated her with a passion. I blocked out Yardi so that I could hear Jaysha and Kanye's conversation from across the room.

"What is wrong with you, Kanye? You don't call me anymore and you have been standing me up lately," Jaysha said to him.

"I keep telling you that I'm not feeling you anymore. Why can't you see that?" he asked her.

"We were in love," she said to him.

"Yeah, until you got pregnant. I can't get you pregnant. That baby wasn't mine, so that just tells me that you stepped out. I'm cool on you, Jaysha. Stop calling my fucking phone. I'm not trying to hurt your feelings, but you are setting yourself up. You slashed my tires, keyed my car, and got the police to pull me over. You are crazy and I don't want any parts of it," Kanye said.

"The baby was yours!" Jaysha said and Kanye laughed in her face. "Human women are very difficult at times. I have never cum inside of you. I can barely fit inside of you. I hope you don't think you can get pregnant by giving head," Kanye said to her.

Jaysha slapped Kanye as hard as she could but I could tell by her expression that it hurt her more than it hurt him. Kanye's body was hard as a brick. A bat burst into the window and attacked Jaysha. The crowd ran out of the frat house while Jaysha screamed and cried as she tried to swat the bat away. The bat bit and scratched at her face before it disappeared.

"What was that?" Yardi asked.

"A bat," I answered. I no longer wanted to be at the party. Hearing Kanye admitting he had feelings for Jaysha turned my stomach. I thought maybe he was just screwing around with her, but he admitted that it was stronger. I kissed Yardi goodbye and promised to call him. I walked out of the house with Baneet and Chancy following behind me.

"What was that about? I know you had something to do with that bat," Chancy said to me.

"I don't know! What is wrong with me?" I asked.

"You've been getting very jealous over Kanye. Yardi can't even keep your attention anymore," Baneet said. I had a slight buzz from the punch and I just wanted to go home.

"This party sucks. Are you two ready to go?" I said to them.

"I'm ready. Hell, I been ready," Baneet said. Jaysha stormed out of the party with her hair all over her head. She bumped into me.

"Move out of my way, bitch!" she said to me.

"Oh no that bitch didn't!" Chancy said. I followed behind Jaysha and we ended up at her car. Before she got in, I grabbed her by the back of her shirt and slammed her into the car.

"Stay away from Kanye and I mean it! If you don't, I will crawl into your window late at night and eat you alive. I will sink my teeth so far into your throat, your neck will snap like a baby bird's leg," I spat. She grabbed at her throat and fell down onto the ground. She coughed up the biggest tarantula I'd ever seen. She burst into tears.

"EEWWWWWWWWWW!" she screamed and I laughed.

"You've been warned," I said and walked away with Baneet and Chancy behind me.

"I want to be a witch, too," Baneet said and Chancy agreed.

"She won't be bothering him anymore," I said.

******

After I got home from the party, I showered and crawled into bed. I tried to sleep but I couldn't. Kanye was on my mind and visions of him thrusting inside of me filled my head. A strong ache formed between my legs. I crawled back out of bed then grabbed my robe.

Seconds later, I stood in front of Kanye's room door. I looked down both ends of the hall and made sure nobody was coming. I disappeared then reappeared inside of his room. Kanye slept peacefully on his back. I blushed at his growls mixed with light snoring. I found him to be fascinating, especially his beast. My eyes roamed over his sculpted chest and tight abs. I slid the covers back and quietly got into his bed. I didn't know why I had those urges but I couldn't help it. I had to be close to him even if it was just for a few seconds. I could see the outline of his dick print through the thin sheet. I had a strong craving for him. A growl almost slipped from my lips, but I hurriedly covered my mouth. Kanye opened his eyes and his ice blue gaze stared at me.

"What in the hell are you doing in my room, Monifa? Your crazy ass better not have cursed me," he said and got out of the bed.

"I was looking for my necklace! I know you took it!" I yelled at him.

"I know you better calm your voice down before your father comes in here and wonders what you are doing here. If I did take your necklace, what makes you think I would sleep with the cheap thing?" he asked.

"I wanted to be sure," I said headed toward his door. Kanye pulled me back then pushed me against the wall. I pushed him back and he held both of my arms above my head. He growled but it wasn't an angry growl because his beast was in lust. He ran his nose down my neck then kissed it. His sharp teeth grazed my skin then sent shivers down my spine. His tongue made a trail down to my breast. My robe came open and I was exposed. He pressed his body into mine and I felt his oversized hard-on. His tongue gently slid across my nipple and his hand found its way between my slit. I was soaking wet and throbbing for him. He pulled away from me.

"Get the fuck out of my room," he spat. He opened up his door then pushed me into the hallway.

"Asshole!" I screamed before he slammed the door in my face. I hurriedly tied up my robe before I headed back to my room. I was aroused and confused. Yardi was very sexual but Kanye did something else to me without touching me. When I walked into my bedroom, my mother was sitting on my bed. She was very, very old but she looked to be in her late twenties. Immortals started aging very slowly once they hit eighteen. The offspring in the pack was Zaan, Kanye, Akea, Chancy, Baneet, and me. We still looked eighteen but we were a few years older.

"What's going on, Mother?" I asked. She patted the bed. I sat down next to her.

"Why were you in Kanye's room?" she asked me.

"I was looking for my necklace," I lied and she laughed.

"Who are you fooling, Monifa? That necklace is the least bit of your concern. You have desires, perhaps, even urges to be with him. Do you sexually crave him? And don't lie because I can see your visions when I want to."

"Yes, I have them. I don't know why, but I do. I can't help it," I admitted and she laughed.

"Your father will kill me if I told you this but Kanye is your soulmate. When you have those desires and feelings for someone that strong, it just means that you two are meant to be," she said.

"Ewwwwwwww," I said.

"You are saying that now. Every day that passes, it will become stronger. I just hate to see when Izra figures it out. He will lose his mind. I need to get ready for the headaches that will come," she said and stood up.

"It's not a good thing to lead someone on, Monifa. I know that you aren't into that human boy. It will never work anyway because you and him are so different. You might want to break it off before he becomes too attached," she said. She kissed my forehead before she walked out of my room. I laid in bed and tossed and turned all night. I should've slept next to Kanye where it was more comfortable.

Akea

I sat at my desk, in my room, studying for an exam for my Astrology class. There was a knock at my bedroom door.

"What is it? I'm busy," I said. The door opened and when I turned around it was Chancy.

"Do you want to go to the movies with me?" she asked me.

"I'm studying," I said.

"Who cares? You need to come out for some air. I want you to go to the movies with me and I'm not leaving your room until you do. I'm going to sit right here," she said and hopped onto my desk. She crossed her legs and arms. Her eyes turned yellow when she looked at me. I dropped my pen.

"Fine, I will go," I said and she hugged me. I stood up then grabbed my jacket. She cleared her throat.

"Sorry, Akea. I said movies not school. I like the look that you go for, you know, the smart clean look, but you need to bring it down just a notch," she said to me.

"You want me to change my clothes?" I asked her.

"Umm, yes that would be nice. Wait right here," she said and walked out of the room. Moments later, she came back with two shopping bags.

"What is that?" I asked her.

"I was doing a little shopping with the girls and I bought something that would look good on you," she said.

"I don't want to dress like Zaan and Kanye," I said and she growled at me.

"You just offended me. I know that and that's what I like about you," she said. She pulled out a pair of nice jeans with a stylish jacket that looked like a blazer with a hood on it. She bought me a pair of loafers to match.

"I like this," I said.

"I know. It's between thug and school boy," she said.

"Let me take a shower and I will be right out," I said and she kissed me and her kiss landed on my lips. When she walked out of the room, I took a shower then got dressed. A half hour later, I walked down the long, spiral staircase. My father came out of the kitchen dressed in business attire. My mother wasn't good at keeping track of how much money the jewelry stores made because it was too much money. My father stepped up and took over the accounts. He fussed about it at first because he had to get up early and go to work, but over the years he got used to it.

"Who is the young lady?" he smirked.

"Chancy," I said.

"Now, son, you are about to cause an uproar in this house because your uncle Dayo is missing a few screws. I might have to kick his ass. Now, when you go out with Chancy, be on good behavior," he said.

"I will," I said.

"Come talk to me for a minute before you leave," he said. I followed him into the family room. He took off his suit jacket and loosened his tie.

"I still have to get used to wearing that hot thing all day," he said. He poured himself a glass of cognac that sat on the table behind the couch.

"It will make me much happier if you connected with your brother. I know you might think that you two are different but you two came from the same womb. You two are identical twins and him being a beast and you being a warlock shouldn't make a difference. I know that he teases you but it's because he wants your attention. I know you like studying and I am a proud father because of that, but your family in this house is important, too," he said.

"Kanye and I have nothing in common, Father," I said. A displeased look came across his face.

"You and your brother are going to get along and I don't mind forcing it," he said in a stern voice. He stood up.

"Have fun tonight," he said and walked out of the living room. Chancy came into the room with her face done up in make-up. She wore a jean, one-piece outfit with a pair of strappy, heeled sandals. Her thick hair was braided straight back into a style. Chancy was very beautiful. She had skin the color of a Hershey's bar. Her eyes slanted in the corners and she had a pair of full, pretty lips. Her cheekbone structure was strong, showing off her Indian roots. She was slimmer than Baneet and Monifa, but she was just as beautiful. She flirted a lot and was a bit wild but her personality could light up the room. Her mother, Anik, and twin sister, Baneet, had an aura about them that made everything seem peaceful.

"Let's go!" she said and pulled me out of the door.

****

Chancy sat in the passenger seat of my car, talking and giggling. I laughed at a few of her jokes.

"You have a beautiful smile, Akea," she said and I looked at her.

"You have one, too," I replied.

"Are you a virgin?" she asked me. I almost swerved my car off the road.

"Ummm, no," I said. She looked at me and crossed her arms.

"You been with someone?" she asked me.

"Yes, a girl that was in my science club," I answered.

"What is her name?" she asked me.

"Sarah, Sarah Baxter," I answered.

"What immortal has a name like that?" she asked.

"She is human," I replied.

We pulled up to the mall. I parked my car and got out to let Chancy out. She grabbed my hand and strutted toward the movie theatre with me following behind. I paid for our tickets then went to the popcorn and candy stand.

"I didn't think I would run into you here," a voice said from behind me. When I turned around, it was Sarah staring at me with her blue eyes.

"The movie is about to start," Chancy said. When she saw Sarah and I looking at each other, she froze.

"You know her or something?" Chancy asked.

"My name is Sarah and we were in the same science club," Sarah replied.

"Ohhhhh, you are Sarah? Ms. Sarah Baxter?" Chancy asked with an attitude.

"Yes, and you are?" Sarah asked as her friends stood behind her, uncomfortable because of Chancy's attitude.

"I'm his girlfriend. Now, let's go, Akea," Chancy spat. She shoved her popcorn and candy in my arms. I looked at Sarah before I followed Chancy.

Chancy didn't say anything to me as we watched the zombie movie. All the other females in the movie theatre snuggled up under their dates. Chancy sat quietly with her eyes straight forward.

"Did I hurt you?" I asked Chancy. Her yellow-brownish eyes stared at me then it turned back to their normal color which was brown.

"Is she the reason why you don't feel comfortable around me? Is it my skin?" she asked me.

"Why would you ask me that?" I asked her.

"Sarah is whiter than my damn popcorn, Akea," Chancy spat.

"It was just something that happened. I think your skin is beautiful," I said and she smiled.

"Kiss me," she said.

"Right now?" I asked.

"Yes, I want you to kiss me," she said. I leaned forward and placed my lips on Chancy's glossed ones. I kissed her and she slipped her tongue inside of my mouth.

Suck on my tongue! Her voice came inside of my head. I gently sucked on her tongue and she pulled away from me. She laid her head on my shoulder. When I looked down the aisle, Sarah and her friends stared at me.

That will teach them bitches not to stare! Chancy said. I had a feeling that Chancy was going to turn my world upside down in a good and bad way.

Osiris

I laid in bed while one of the servants rubbed my back. My father had me training for a whole day to become a great warrior. I was the son of King Baki and Queen Jalesa of Anubi. My aunt Meda came into my room. She sent the servant away.

"What do you want, Meda?" I asked her. Meda is my father's sister. Rumor around Anubi is that an old warlock got inside of her mother's womb. Meda's mother died when she gave birth to her and my father raised her. I was born a year after Meda was born. She was like my sister instead of my aunt. She pulled a globe out of her pocket.

"What is that?" I asked her.

"This is Earth. The place where your uncle Goon lives. He is Ammon's second son; the black wolf. He killed my father," she said.

"Ammon was a bad wolf and made Anubi a bad place. Watch how you speak!" I said to her and she laughed.

"You are brainwashed but I will not be. Ammon was a great warrior. Drawings of him are all over this temple," she said.

"That was before greed and power killed him. I don't care anything about Ammon or Earth," I replied.

"I want to show you something," she said. I followed Meda through the temple and into her sanctuary. She closed the door and locked it behind me. She told me to have a seat and I sat down across from her.

"I have something that will make you stronger. You will not need to train so much," she said. She sat a cup down in front of me.

"What is that?" I asked her as I sniffed it.

"Water from the Nile River. That's the river Goon drank from and he became stronger. He is even stronger than your father's beast," she said.

She sat the globe down in front of me and showed me a big black beast with blue eyes. I picked up the globe and watched the black beast run through the woods. His beast was strong and had the strength of ten warriors.

"I have never seen anything like it," I said to Meda.

"His eyes are the color of the Nile River because he drank the water," she replied.

"I didn't hear that story," I replied.

"That's because Anubi doesn't want us to know everything. This place holds many secrets. Now, drink the water so you can be strong like your uncle," she said to me. I pushed the cup away.

"I will do it the right way as my father did. He practiced every day and so will I," I said. I stood up and walked toward the door but she blocked me in.

"What are you doing?" I asked when I turned around. Meda stared at me with glowing eyes.

"I didn't want to force it but now I have to," she said. She used a force to hold me down. I tried to shift but I couldn't. My growls were muffled out.

"You are such a fool," she said. She grabbed a bat from a cage in the corner of her room. It made noises as she carried it over to me.

"Back in the dark times in Egypt, our gods were cat people and werewolf people. Everyone worshipped the two but there was another god nobody spoke of. It was a god that sucked the blood out of a human's life. The warriors captured him because they feared him. They thought he was the devil because he couldn't stand daylight. He was very different from the other two gods because he didn't shift into a beast. The warriors held him out in the sun where his body turned to ash. His ashes were kept in an urn and I found it. It was in the dungeon downstairs in this temple. I gave him life from those ashes through this bat. This bat will bite you then kill you. Your heart will not beat anymore and your beast will be no more. You will be reborn as a vampire. You will be casted away to Earth because Anubi will fear you. I wonder how your coward father will feel about his only son being a vampire. It's nothing against you, my wrath is against your father and all that he stands for. He watched my father die and did nothing, and now he will watch his son hunt and feed on his own people," Meda said to me. The bat latched onto my neck and sucked the life out of me until I stopped breathing...

Kanye

The sound of the branches breaking underneath my paw echoed through the woods. I was hunting for a snack. My appetite was growing and I found myself eating two deer a day. My father had a bigger appetite than I did. He and I ate more than any wolf from our pack. I think it was because of our strong warrior genes. We were also bigger wolves, and even though my wolf was still considered a pup, I was almost my father's size. I sniffed the air because I was not in the woods alone. A light growl came from behind me and I turned around. Monifa's eyes glowed as she stared at me. She was still in human form but because of her canines I knew she wanted to shift.

Can I hunt in peace? I asked her.

"Yes, you can, but your stench is stinging my nose. When was the last time you bathed your wolf?" she asked.

Very funny coming from the puppy that invaded my room the other night, I replied. A small bolt of electricity came from the tip of her fingers. She was mad at me but that was the usual. We never got along and the older we got, the worse it got. I shifted in human form and stood in front of her naked. I growled at her and she backed up. I sniffed the air and walked closer to her. Her scent was driving my beast wild. It was a musty but sweet scent that poured from between her legs. It caused my dick to ache and the bottom of my stomach cramped.

"Step back and away from me," she said. I stepped closer to her and her scent grew stronger. She was aroused and so was I but I couldn't understand why our bodies wanted each other because we couldn't get along. I ripped her shirt open and her breasts sat up perfectly. A light growl came from the pit of my stomach. The sounds of her breathing picked up and I wanted to take her but I couldn't. I punched the tree next to me and pieces of the bark flew off.

"Get out of the woods before my beast takes advantage of you!" I yelled at her. Her eyes trailed down to the erection that hung between my legs. Pre-cum oozed from the tip of my dick and her eyes changed again. A whimper escaped her lips.

"What is happening to us?" she cried.

"I don't know," I spat.

"Our bodies are trying to connect but we don't want them to," she said.

"Can I finish hunting? Everyone knows that I don't like to hunt with anyone. I like to do it alone because it gives me a peace of mind. There's too many of us and I can never think to myself around everyone," I said.

"I can hear what you're thinking anyway whether it's close by or miles away," she teased.

"That's because you are an evil witch," I replied. She leaped on me and dug her nails into my face.

"Don't call me that, asshole!" she screamed and bit my shoulder. I howled because her sharp teeth tore into my flesh. I rolled her over onto her back and choked her. My skin pulled together to close up the wound on my shoulder.

"Don't you ever bite me again, witch," I spat and let her go. A lightning bolt struck me in the chest and my body flew into a tree. I stood up and snapped my back into place.

"Your witchcraft isn't a match for my beast. However, it's very cute," I teased and headed in the other direction. She tried to attack me from the back but I turned around and caught her in mid-air.

"Stop, damn. What is up with you?" I asked.

"I hate you!" she screamed. I tossed her over onto my back then climbed up a tree.

"Keep still. You know your ass is heavy. You might need to lay off the cows you be sneaking out to eat," I said.

I jumped from tree to tree with her hanging on until I got to the big lake that was on our land. On the other side of the lake, there was a family of deer. I dropped Monifa down on the ground.

"Go hunt," I said. She stood up and brushed her pants off.

"Go hunt? We are wolves, not lions! The female doesn't hunt for the males. Learn your animal kingdom, jackass," she fussed.

"I figure you owe me," I said and she smirked.

"I hate you." I laughed because she told me every second how much she hated me. Her cell phone rang in her back pocket. She pulled it out to look at and I snatched it from her.

"Give me my phone back!" she yelled and the deer ran.

"Look what you did. Now, I have to chase one," I said. I answered her phone.

"What's up?" I asked Yardi.

"Where is Monifa and why are you answering her phone, Kanye? I thought we had this discussion before," he said with venom dripping from his voice.

"And I thought when we had this discussion the last time, I cleared everything up for you. Monifa is always around me and you know that," I replied. I traced my finger down the side of her cheek and she stood with her arms crossed with a scowl on her face. She knew she wasn't a match for me because every time she was around, I ended up with her phone.

"What is going on between the two of you?" he shouted.

"Nigga, stop acting like a bitch in human life," I said and laughed.

"You can have her. Fuck her and you, too!" he shouted and hung up the phone.

"Your human pet just broke up with you. I would apologize if I cared," I said.

"I don't think I care myself," she said and sat down in the grass. She let out a deep breath.

"It's hard being in love with a human. I love him but the connection in our bodies isn't there. The sex is not what I imagined. He's not lacking in that department but he just cannot fulfil my desires," she said.

"You need wolf dick, that's all," I replied and she rolled her eyes.

"Get your mind out of the gutta for once and try to hold a normal conversation. Everything doesn't have to be ignorant," she said.

"It's not being ignorant. It's called being blunt and not sugarcoating shit. You need your own kind to fuck you. To expand between your walls and bite you until your body feels like it's floating," I replied.

"I did my research and when a female human loses her virginity, her hymen is broken and it bleeds. My hymen is still intact. I should've known then that Yardi and I couldn't work," she said sadly. I sat down next to her. The sun started to hide behind the clouds. The woods were pretty at night, especially when the light from the moon and the stars casted upon the lake.

"If it makes you feel any better, a human can't satisfy me, either. The urge is there but the pleasure isn't. I can't fit into them. We need to stick to our own kind," I replied.

"My mother told me that you and I are destined to be together. I don't want to believe it but with each day that passes, I'm starting to. Your scent wakes me up out of my sleep and you've been agitating me really bad lately. Maybe we should have sex so the urge can go away," she said.

"Is that why you followed me into the woods? You want me to please you?" I asked.

"I want to get it over with so my urge can go away," she replied.

"Izra will kill me."

"My father won't know. The urges are bad and it won't go away until we do it," she said. She slowly stood up and got undressed. Seconds later, she stood before me naked. Her scent poured out of her pores and her eyes glowed. Black, sharp nails expanded from her fingertips, and a light growl escaped her lips. She almost seemed possessed. Monifa hated my guts but she wanted me inside of her. A sticky-like drizzle dripped from between her legs.

Come here, I said.

She walked closer to me and her scent pulled me into her. I gripped her by the hips with my nails digging into her skin. I sniffed her like an animal—like a wild beast. I traced my nose up and down her slit and she whined. I gently bit her swollen bud before I latched onto her pussy. She howled and the birds flew out of the trees. I pulled her down and she straddled my face. My long tongue entered her tight and dripping hole. I was buried in her scent and my dick hardened. It hardened like it never had before.

"Kanyeeeeee," she chanted my name. Her body swayed side-to-side like she was under a spell—she was hypnotized. Her vaginal lips moved seductively on my tongue. My nails dug in her ass cheeks. She bucked her hips forward and screamed my name. Her body trembled when my tongue moved faster in and out of her. She growled and whimpered when she bounced up and down on my tongue. She was having another orgasm. It was natural for us to know a woman's body, even if it's our first time having sex. Werewolves are sexual and we connect a lot during intercourse. We didn't have to do human things like dating and getting to know one another. Sex was more than pleasure because it was our way to connect spiritually. My father taught me about it when I slept with my first human.

Pre-cum drizzled from my shaft and I couldn't hold back any longer. I pulled her down onto the ground and rolled over on top of her. My tongue traced the outline of her neck as I fondled her swollen breast. My teeth sank into her nipple and she bit my neck. I growled at her and she bit me harder. Her legs wrapped around me and her nails dug into my back while I sucked on her hard, dark nipple.

Enter me! she yelled inside of my head. I traced my dick between her slit and pushed my way in.

"FUCK!" I shouted out because she bit me. She was tight—very tight. I howled out when I continued to fill her up. I felt her hymen rip and she cried.

It's too big! It's too big! she yelled inside of my head. I kissed her to ease the pain but I couldn't pull out even if I wanted to. My beast was stubborn and I wanted it as much as her, if not more. I went deeper and she moaned louder. My back cracked and my neck snapped. My beast wanted to come out as I expanded inside of her. I stretched her open more and she couldn't close her legs if she wanted to. I was deep inside of her—too deep. I pumped in and out of her and her body slid up and down in the grass. Her eyes rolled to the back of her head and her face grew into a snout. Her beast wanted to come out, too, but two beasts having sex was deadly. We could've hurt each other if we didn't control it. A puddle seeped from between her legs. I went harder and faster and my dick swelled again. It swelled up and I couldn't move in and out of her the way I wanted to. I howled before I bit her nipple. I bit her too hard because I tasted her blood inside of my mouth. I clamped down onto her breast like it was a raw steak. It looked like it hurt but she received an orgasmic high from me marking her. She stopped breathing and I burst inside of her. It was the best feeling in the world. Monifa was able to take all of my beast. I collapsed on top of her and fell asleep.

****

I woke up to the sounds of birds chirping. I felt something underneath me. When I looked down, Monifa was lying under me asleep.

"Oh shit!" I called out. She was snoring and a cute growl escaped her lips. I shook her.

"Wake up!"

"Go away! Why are you in my bedroom?" she asked and rolled over on her side. She looked around and sat up. She covered her breasts and her pussy.

"What happened? Why are we here?" she asked.

"We fucked in the woods. Now get up so we can go back home. I know the pack is looking for us," I said. She stood up and she had a marking on her back. The same tribal marking as me.

"Oh shit," I said. Izra was going to know I marked his daughter.

"What happened?" she asked me.

"You are going to need a lot of magic to get that marking off your back," I said.

"Why did you do it?" she asked and punched me in the arm.

"I didn't. It's a tradition I guess," I replied. She grabbed her clothes and stormed off. She disappeared into the woods.

****

When I walked inside of our house, it was empty. I showered and got dressed for school. I didn't want to go but I knew my father would've been pissed. It wasn't hard to piss him off because he had a bad temper and a lot of days everyone stayed clear of him. It was a part of his beast and it was uncontrollable, so we had to deal with it. After I left the house, I got inside of my car and sped off. Thirty minutes later, I was pulling up on campus. When I got out of my car, Yardi and his football friends were standing outside of the building.

"You like to talk shit over the phone?" he asked me.

"Nigga, what is this supposed to be? Some type of intervention? Back the fuck up or I will turn into something that will scare all of you punk muthafuckas," I spat.

"Stay away from Monifa," he said. I stepped closer to him and whispered in his ear.

"I wouldn't have a problem with it if she didn't explode on my dick last night," I said and he pushed me. I slammed him onto a car and choked him.

"This is your last warning. I'm trying to save your life," I said before I pulled away from him. I picked my backpack up off the ground and walked into the building. His friends threatened me behind my back but I ignored it. My biggest fear was shifting in front of humans. Another reason I didn't want to go to college was because I was short-tempered like my father. When I walked to my first class, Daja was leaned against the wall by the door. She was a werewolf, too, but from another pack. Her scent was alluring but my beast still didn't crave her. Daja was brown-skinned and she wore her hair in braids. She was cute and petite and had the prettiest set of golden-hazel eyes.

"I was wondering if you wanted to hang out tonight?" she asked.

"It depends on what we are hanging out for," I said and she blushed. She was aroused and I knew what she wanted; she wanted me to seduce her. She was attracted to my scent. I had a strong scent that alpha males possessed. My father was the alpha of the pack but I was next in line.

"I think you got the idea," she said and a light growl escaped her lips.

Jerk! Monifa's voice yelled in my head.

What are you doing in my head? We are not by each other! Is this a part of witchcraft? I asked.

I don't know. I've been hearing your thoughts all morning. Are you going to go out with Daja? Ugh, she isn't pretty. I'm starting to believe that you'll screw anything, Monifa ranted.

Mind your business. I gave you what you wanted, now get the hell out of my head! I replied.

I hate you! she said.

"Are you okay?" Daja asked me.

"Yeah, I'm fine. I will see you later," I said and walked into class.

****

Hours later...

"You and Monifa did what?" Zaan asked me. We were on the basketball court inside of our house.

"We fucked and now I'm connected to her," I said.

"Bro, what were you thinking? Izra is going to kill you," he said.

"Dayo is going to kill you for screwing Baneet, so we'll die together," I said and he chuckled.

"What's going on?" Amadi asked when he stepped onto the court. He was wearing basketball shorts and a tank top. He was an old werewolf like my father but he didn't look a day over thirty-four.

"Just shooting the breeze. What's up with you? Ula let you out of her sight?" I joked.

"Very funny, pup. Ula doesn't control me, understand?" he asked.

"Yeah right, Unc. Ula controls everything you do," Zaan said.

"When you get older, you will learn how to appreciate the spirit of your soulmate. But in the bedroom, she lets my beast tame her. That's all that matters," Amadi replied.

"Damn," Zaan said.

"Are y'all shooting hoops without me?" Dayo asked when he came into the gym. I looked at Zaan and he looked nervous.

Don't get nervous now, nigga. Yo' stepdaddy is about to bite that ass, I teased him.

Shut up before he hears our thoughts if he hasn't already, Zaan replied. After we played basketball, we all went hunting. I needed to figure out a way to hide my scent that was on Monifa before Izra figured it out. He went on a trip to Africa along with Elle and Elle's mate, Fabia which is Zaan's mother.

I need one of Amadi's oils, I thought.

Monifa

Baneet, Chancy, and I were sitting in the nail place getting our nails done. It was a stupid idea because every time we shifted, the polish on our nails cracked. After I told them I slept with Kanye, they couldn't believe how easily I let him have me. They thought I hated him but I wondered to myself if I ever really did.

"You heard him talking to Daja? That is amazing how you two are connected. But we can go and kick her ass," Chancy said.

"You always want to kick ass. Why can't you be like Baneet?" I joked.

"Because Baneet is boring. Besides, I need to kick some ass to relieve some stress. Akea doesn't like our kind," she said.

"He is an immortal. Why wouldn't he?" I asked.

"I don't mean that kind. I meant our damn skin, Monifa. He's in love with Miss Sarah Baxter. You should see her, she has long, blonde hair and pretty blue eyes. She's nice and slim and she flicks her hair over her shoulder when she's trying to be cute," Chancy fussed.

"I'm not surprised. Akea is a little more to himself," I said.

"Most definitely but find another immortal to date. Matter of fact, there is this Underground party tonight where all the werewolves will be. We should go and find you a beast," Baneet said and Chancy rolled her eyes.

"I don't want a beast. I want a warlock and his name is Akea. I don't want to be bitten during sex. I heard it was painful," Chancy said.

"Was it painful?" Baneet asked me.

"Yes, very painful, but it made me see another world. I got a glimpse of Anubi while I was cumming. I saw ancient pyramids and I saw Goon's ancient beast," I said.

"That's because Goon's blood flows through his sons. They see the past life the same way Goon does. Kanye and Akea have ancient royalty blood, blood from the gods," Baneet said. After our nails dried, we headed out of the nail salon and into the parking lot. All of a sudden, a burning sensation shot up my back and it knocked me down onto the ground.

"Get it off me! Get it off! Something is crawling under my skin and it burns!" I screamed while I rolled around on the ground. Chancy lifted up my shirt.

"You have a tribal marking circling around the one you showed us this morning. Everyone will know that Kanye marked you. You two are doomed," she said. Tears came down my eyes and Baneet picked me up and tossed me over her shoulder. She took off running toward the woods. Female werewolves were stronger than a human men—a lot stronger.

"I smell a pond nearby so hold on," she said. When we came to the pond, she dropped me into the water. The cold water was soothing and I almost fell asleep. I was very weak and barely had the energy to teleport.

"She's weak," Chancy said when she caught up to us.

"Kanye should've wore a muzzle," Baneet said.

"I know we are a part of the dog species but are you freakin' serious? That is so animalistic," Chancy said.

"We are animals and if he would've wore one, he wouldn't have marked her. Zaan and I do it all the time. It's like our condom if you ask me. During sex he wants to bite me and mark me but he can't," Baneet said.

"That doesn't make any sense. Are you telling me you two are cheating the connection we are supposed to have within our tradition? You gave your body to him but he can still mark another wolf," Chancy fussed.

"You two cut it out, please," I said.

"I'm not listening to her because she doesn't know how it feels. She wants someone who doesn't even look at her in that way," Baneet spat. Chancy growled at her and Baneet growled back. I slowly crawled out of the pond and fell down into the dirt. Baneet and Chancy shifted into their beasts and attacked each other. Their beasts were brown and white and they both possessed tribal markings of Egyptian roots and Anik's Indian roots. Their markings were red and black. Chancy's wolf had a red dot in between her eyes. Baneet's wolf had red at the tip of her ears. That was the only way I could tell their beasts apart. I used the little bit of strength I gained to separate them with a bolt of electricity. I growled at them.

"STOP IT!" I cried. I was emotional because my body was changing and my pack sisters were fighting. They shifted back and both stood in front of me naked. Baneet had three long, deep scratches going down her face. Chancy was more of a fighter and her beast overpowered Baneet's. I didn't understand it myself because in human form, Baneet is bigger than Chancy, but my father told me that our beast is separate from us.

"We are sorry," Baneet said and helped me up.

"We need to figure out a way to get to the car without being spotted naked," Chancy said.

"I have extra clothes in my tote bag," I said and we fell out into laughter. We took turns carrying extra clothes because things got out of hand sometimes.

****

I laid in bed with my headphones on, listening to rap music while I studied for my test. I sniffed the air and growled because Kanye was near and he was too close.

What do you want? I asked him.

Open up the door. We need to talk and it's important, he said. I looked at the door and it opened. I used my witchcraft more than I used my beast. Kanye walked in and his scent caused a moan to escape my lips. Wetness seeped from between my legs and his eyes turned ice blue. He could smell my arousal.

"Make it quick because I don't have much to say to you," I said.

"What I do?" he asked.

"We shared a special moment last night and as much as I hate you, I thought you would've at least cherished it, too. I gave you my beast and as soon as you saw Daja, you wanted to fuck her! I heard your thoughts and you think she is cute and you want to feel her pretty lips wrapped around your dick. I heard it all, Kanye," I fussed.

"Coming from someone who is with a human," he spat.

"What did you come in here for?" I asked. He dropped a bottle of oil on my bed.

"Soak in this before my scent on you becomes stronger and everyone will know we had sex," he said. My heart almost shattered into a million pieces.

I'm not good enough for him. He doesn't want me to smell like him. He wants to forget about something that was so beautiful to me. The way he felt inside of me came from another world. It was more beautiful than magic, I thought. I didn't want to have those feelings for him but they came naturally. It didn't feel forced, it felt like it was meant to be. I understood the spiritual connection my mother was talking about. It was getting harder and harder for me to resist him. Why did he have to be so handsome? Why did his beast have to be overpowering?

"Get the fuck out of room and do it now," I said. I felt myself shifting.

"Your beast wants to challenge me?" he asked. I sent him sailing across the room and he ended up in my bathroom. I crawled up the wall and my teeth sharpened.

Calm down! I yelled inside of my head. All of our beasts had a different personality and my beast had one, a major one. My beast was a jealous beast. I knew what I had to do. I burst out of the window and in mid-air I shifted. I ran through the woods and across the highway. A car almost swerved off the road and the driver honked its horn. I roamed through the woods on another wolf's territory. Minutes later, I was on Daja's pack's land.

I was breaking werewolf rules but rules are made to broken. She wanted Kanye and she wanted him to mate with her. Female wolves without tradition were promiscuous. They mated with any male wolf just for the feeling of the bite. The male bite was like a drug to us—an addiction. I howled outside of her house. She and a guy that she resembled walked out of the small, white, brick house and their yellow eyes glowed in the dark. Daja's bones snapped and she crouched over; she was shifting into her beast. After she shifted, she shook the shreds of clothing off her body. Her brother shifted and growled at me. Their beasts were brown with a white stripe going down the middle of their backs.

What are you doing on our territory? Daja asked.

I didn't come here to fight but I will if I have to. I came here to warn you. Stay the hell away from Kanye or else I will cast a spell on you and your entire pack. I will send your soul into the pits of hell, I spat.

I will not stay away from him. He is a single wolf until he mates and has pups. Screwing and mating are not the same. I will carry his pups and you will be forgotten, she teased. I growled at her before I charged into her. Her brother bit me and I howled but it didn't stop me from sinking my teeth into Daja's throat. I tossed her up in the air and her body slammed into a tree. She whimpered when she stood up and blood dripped from the wound on her neck. Her brother tried to charge me again but I used my magic to knock him into a tree and I shielded myself. He tried to charge into me again and was electrocuted by the force I had over me.

You've been warned, bitch, I threatened her. More wolves came out of the woods. Their eyes glowed and their scowls showed their sharp teeth. There were six wolves total, including Daja and her brother. My shield couldn't hold them all off but I wasn't scared of a challenge.

You came on our territory, bitch! Daja spat. Then I heard the sounds of loud growling and branches in the woods snapping. The scent was too familiar. A black paw with gold tips stepped out of the woods. He was massive and his mane was black as night. The beast had a gold diamond-shaped pattern between its ice blue eyes. Gold was at the tips of his ears and his canines were made of gold. He stepped completely out of the woods and the other wolves backed away. Kanye's beast was beautiful. He inherited the gold from Kanya's jackal and the midnight black from Goon. He looked at the wolves and growled.

We will leave peacefully, he said to Daja's brother.

She came on our land and wounded our sister. Do you think because you are rich and come from Gods that you can do what you want? You still have to follow the rules! We don't bother your land, so don't bother ours or else we will be forced to kill, he said to Kanye.

We will leave peacefully. If you want to fight, let her go and I will fight for her, but this will end. If we leave peacefully, we will never come back, Kanye said. He spoke like a true alpha. Zaan and the twins came from out of the bushes with scowls on their faces. Zaan's beast was white with black markings. Kanye always teased him and called him a zebra. In Anubi's history, a white beast meant "great warrior."

Take the bitch and get off of our land, her brother said. Kanye growled at her brother and he backed up. Kanye's scowl was menacing—very menacing. Daja growled at me. I turned around and headed back to the woods. Kanye was mad at me and his beast growled at me the whole way home. Zaan, Baneet, and Chancy didn't say a word to me, either.

If my father doesn't know about this, we will not say anything about it, Kanye said. I was embarrassed that I let jealousy consume me. Chancy went inside of the house. Zaan and Baneet disappeared into the night. I walked into woods on the opposite side of the house and shifted back to my human form.

"What is your problem?" Kanye asked me.

"You are too selfish to understand," I said with my back toward him. He walked closer to me and touched the new marking I had on my back that matched his. I grabbed his hand and we disappeared into my bedroom. We were standing in my bedroom naked. I pulled him closer to me with my breasts pressed against his solid chest. He picked me up and I wrapped my legs around him. I wasn't in control and neither was he. Our bodies wanted each other and there was nothing we could do about it. He entered his massive dick inside of me and I wanted to howl but he covered my mouth. My nails dug into his shoulders while he bounced me up and down on his dick. I was dripping wet and my wetness splashed onto the floor. I bit him and he grew inside of me. I wanted to be locked away from the world at that moment. I just wanted it to be us two.

A few hours later, after we made love, I laid on my side and Kanye laid next to me with his strong arms holding me. He sucked on my neck and growled.

"You are a big puppy," I said and laughed.

"Shut up, Monifa," he said and gently bit me. He was a jerk—a big jerk but I over exaggerated it. He wasn't as bad as I pretended he was.

****

Two days later...

I walked around the two-level condo which was located a half hour away from the mansion. I wanted a place to myself.

"How much is the rent?" I asked the realtor.

"It's two thousand a month. You are a college student. Are you sure this is something you want to do?" the Caucasian middle-aged woman asked me.

"I will pay up to a year in cash today if you can get me the keys," I said and she smiled.

"Great. I'm going to go to my car and get the paperwork," she said and left the condo. I looked out of the window and it had a nice city view.

"Not bad. Not bad at all," a voice said from behind me. When I turned around, I came face-to-face with my mother.

"What are you doing here?" I asked.

"Well, for starters, you took a large amount of money out of me and your father's safe. I know you have a huge shopping habit but there was something off about this. You are becoming distant, you are moody, and Kanye's attitude went from bad to horrible. He is almost as bad as his father. You two marked each other," she said.

"I didn't mean for it to happen," I replied.

"It's in our nature," she said and walked around admiring the appliances and cherry wood floors.

"When a mother is ready to give birth, she becomes more independent. She wants to provide for her pups and she becomes possessive," she said.

"I'm not pregnant," I said.

"Not yet, but your body wants you to be. After your soulmate marks your body for the first time, it prepares your body for pups. You will go into heat soon. After you mate, you will be tied to Kanye for life," she said.

"I don't want to become a mother," I said. I almost wanted to faint. My life was rapidly changing.

"Our lives from our ancestors are already mapped out. What's happening now is meant to happen. Let me see your back," she said. I turned around and she lifted my shirt. She traced her fingers over my markings.

"Izra will fall over and die. I don't know what to do. You are his only pup and he holds you close to his heart, but the good side of it is that I'm going to be a grandparent," she said and smiled.

"Why are you smiling?" I asked.

"I can't have any more babies but you can. I will get to experience it through my grandbabies. This is exciting," she said.

"Seriously, Mother?"

"I can't cry about it. We can't cheat fate. Why not embrace it because at the end of it all, you are still destined to be with Kanye," she said.

"I don't know what to tell Father when he comes back from his trip with Elle," I said.

"We have a few days to figure it out," she replied.

Osiris

I woke up in my bed and my vision was blurry. I felt weak and starved.

"What's going on with me?" I asked out loud. The last thing I remembered was my aunt Meda showing me a bat. I held my head as I stumbled around in my room. I tripped over my feet and came crashing down onto the floor.

"What a shame," my aunt's voice echoed throughout the room.

"What did you do to me? What did you do? I feel empty!" I yelled at her and she laughed. Someone knocked on the door.

"Is everything okay in there, prince?" a warrior that guarded my room asked me. He pushed the door open and ran over to me.

"Are you okay?" he asked and he helped me up. The sound of his pulse beating echoed loudly in my ears like drums. My chest tightened and I felt my teeth breaking through my gums. My teeth were like daggers. They were different than my beast's teeth. The teeth I had coming through my gums were short and sharp—very sharp.

Eat so you can be strong, Meda's voice came inside my head. My head started spinning and I opened my mouth. I grabbed the warrior and bit into his neck and the warm, sweet, tangy blood quenched my thirst.

"GUH... GUH," was the sound the warrior made as he fought to breathe. After I was finished drinking his blood, I snapped his neck so he could no longer suffer. I stood up with blood dripping from my mouth and down the jewels I had around my neck. I picked up the warrior and tossed him out of the window that was inside of my temple. His body splashed into the water.

****

"Your water is ready," a peasant said to me. She was attractive and her breasts were perfectly nice. My father told me that our women were like gems and to treat them as such. But I wanted something else.

Vampires are very sexual and charming immortals. Take full advantage of it, Meda's voice said inside my head. I pulled the silk curtain back and pressed my body against the scared woman's body. I traced my finger down her face.

"Don't be afraid, beautiful," I said and looked into her eyes. She was hypnotized.

"Take everything off and join me for my bath."

She took her clothes off and I grabbed her hand. She stepped down the three stairs and into the pool of bath water. I pulled her close to me and my hands went to her bottom. I wrapped her leg around me and entered her.

"UGH!" she moaned. I pumped in and out her. The urge to bite came again. I kissed her neck and traced my tongue along her pulse. The sound of it beating caused me to explode inside of her. I pulled her braid back and exposed her neck. She was climaxing and her nipples were pressed against my chest like pebbles. The water splashed out of the tub when I sped up. I sank my teeth into her neck and she tried to scream.

Let me, I said into her mind as my eyes pleaded with hers. She stopped fighting me and sacrificed her blood to me. Once I was finished with her, I dragged her out of the tub. I regretted killing her but I couldn't control my hunger.

****

"Turn me back!" I yelled at Meda when I walked into her temple. She closed her spell book and smiled at me.

"Why would I give you a favor if you haven't done anything for me yet? When you ask a witch for a favor, you must do something for it," she said.

"What do you want me to do?" I asked and she smiled.

"Go to Earth and build an army," she said.

"I don't have the ability to do that."

"Werewolves cannot detect vampires. Vampires don't have a scent. They'll never know what you are. Go to Earth and meet your uncle Goon. Find out his pack's weakness and your army will destroy them. You will avenge my father's death and I will turn you back into a werewolf," she said.

"He will question my scent," I replied.

"I can trust that you will think of something. Vampires are good liars," she said.

"My parents will look for me," I replied.

"I have a spell for that. Now, do as I say and I will grant you your wish."

"My skin doesn't like the sun anymore," I said.

"The more blood you drink, the stronger you will become. Follow me," she said.

She pushed back the stone wall inside of her sanctuary and walked down the dark stairwell. I followed behind her. The only light inside of the dungeon was from the fire torches that hung on the brick wall.

"What is this?" I asked.

"Dinner," she said. I looked around the dungeon that held a ton of prisoners.

"By the time you finish feeding on them, you'll have the strength to do a lot of things. Blood is the source that holds your power," she said.

"I'm a murderer," I replied and she smiled.

"So is your father and uncle. Ammon didn't deserve to die. He was the ruler of Anubi and his son killed him while your father watched. Shame on them and they will pay. Baki is paying for it now because his only son is against him and the people of Anubi. Now, drink up and don't be too long," she said and disappeared. I looked around and a lot of eyes stared back at me. She trapped them in a cursed dungeon where they couldn't shift into beasts.

"Please don't do it. You are the son of Baki. You are the good prince of Anubi," one man pleaded.

"Not anymore," I replied and pulled him through the bars. Screams filled my ears as I feasted on the people—the people of Anubi.

****

Two days later...

I fixed the bag I had on my back. Meda had been watching the humans on Earth on her globe and she knew a lot about them. I was dressed in clothes that I wasn't comfortable in. I kept my gold jewelry on from Anubi. I stepped out into the street and what Meda referred to as a "car" almost hit me. The driver swerved and stopped the car. He got out and walked over to me.

"Move out the fuckin' road next time, nigga! You could've gotten killed," he said.

"I don't understand," I said.

"That accent. I know that accent," he said.

"I'm not from around here," I replied.

"Stay out of the road or get ran over. It's your choice," he said and got back inside of the car and drove away.

That was Goon's son, Kanye. You need to learn the way of living on Earth! If you keep acting like that, it will look suspicious! she yelled in my head.

Minutes later, Meda was in my head telling me what to do and how to answer the man that was standing up talking in what he called a "class". Meda called him a "professor". She used some of her magic to get me into the school. I had an Earth identity, too. I was her puppet until I gave her what she wanted.

"It's okay. This class is boring anyway," a sultry voice said from behind me. When I turned around, there was the prettiest creature I had ever seen.

"My name is Chancy. What is your name? You have a unique accent," she said.

"Osiris, Prince of—" Meda yelled in my head.

Don't tell her you are from Anubi! Just tell her Egypt!

Get out of my head, so I can concentrate!

Blood sucker, she teased.

"Excuse me, beautiful, but I'm from Egypt," I said.

"Cool, my dad is, too. I've been there a few times and the pyramids are beautiful," she said. After class was over, I followed Chancy out into the hallway. The sound of her heart beating kept teasing me but I ignored it. It was time for me to feed but she was too beautiful to become a meal.

"Hey, Chancy, there you are. I've been looking all over for you," said another beautiful creature. She was full around her hips like the women in Anubi. She had a body like a marked female wolf by the way her breasts sat up— round and full.

"Monifa, this is Osiris. Osiris, this is my cousin Monifa," Chancy said.

"It's nice to meet you and I love that necklace. The diamonds remind me of the diamonds our family sells at Beastly Treasures," Monifa said to me.

"He is from Egypt and I'm assuming he is not familiar with the area. We should take him out tonight. It'll be fun," Chancy said.

"I have plans tonight so I will take a raincheck but Baneet might go with you," Monifa replied.

"Baneet and Zaan are going out. I guess we are on our own, but I will see you in the cafeteria," Chancy replied before Monifa walked away.

"Come on, Osiris. I'm going to show you around and you can tell me all about Egypt," she said.

Jezebel! Meda spat.

Ancient witch, I replied.

"Everyone around me is in love. What about you? Do you have a mate? I mean a significant other?" she asked. I didn't respond, I just stared at her. I wished she could came back to Anubi with me.

Your thoughts are blocked from her because you are a vampire. I'm only in your head because I put a spell on you. We are connected. Drink a human's blood so you can become more like them. Remember, whomever you drink from, you become, Meda said.

GO AWAY! I replied.

"I don't have what you call a significant other. Do you?" I asked.

"No. We are sorta like dating but I don't think he is interested in me that way. I kinda forced him to like me," she said and giggled.

I like you, I thought. I followed Chancy to a black car.

"Let's go on a city tour," she said.

"You are not afraid of being alone with me?" I asked.

"I can defend myself, trust me. I don't fear anything," she said and I believed her. I stood on the outside of the car and waited for it open.

"You have to open the door. Look, I will show you," she said and opened it for me. I sat in the car and looked around. I didn't understand any of it. She got inside and pressed a button and music played that hurt my ears.

"What kind of music is that?" I asked and she laughed.

"Hardcore rap. I love it," she said.

"What's pussy and ass?" I asked trying to understand the music.

"Pussy is a female's vagina and ass is this," she said and patted her behind. My eyes roamed over the curves of her body and it was the only time I wasn't mad about being a vampire. If I was a beast, I would've lost control of myself. My shaft in my pants hardened and my fangs penetrated through my gums. I needed intimacy and I didn't care who I received it from.

"Are you okay?" she asked and I nodded my head.

Control it! I said to myself. She pulled off and sped through the parking lot on campus. She turned the music up and started moving to the beat.

"Sing it with me! Don't be such a prude," she said.

"I don't like it. It's not like the music back home," I said.

"You'd better get used to it because when we go to the clubs, this is all that plays. I love dancing and I'm actually in a dance class. I have a show coming up and you should check it out. I dance to different music. It takes my mind off of things," she said.

****

Me and Chancy hung out for a bit. We sat in what she called a "Café" and ate dinner but I wasn't hungry for that. Food sickened my stomach. We talked a lot, well, she did all of the talking because I didn't have much to tell and I couldn't tell her what I was. After she finished eating her partially raw burger, we left the Café.

"It's getting late and I should head home. Do you want me to take you somewhere?" she asked.

"No, I'm fine. I don't live far, I can walk. I will see you in school tomorrow," I said. I kissed her cheek and the sound of her heart beating tightened my chest. I needed to feed.

"Okay, see ya!" she said and we went our separate ways. I walked down the street passed the eating places and I heard a noise coming from between the buildings. I disappeared into the dark shadows between the buildings and someone was sitting on the ground, drinking out of a bottle. The person was a man—a very dirty man.

"Do you have any change you can spare?" he asked. I grabbed him by the throat and held him up against the wall. My long thumbnail punctured a hole in his neck as he struggled to get away. The smell of fresh blood filled my nostrils and my fangs expanded. He tried to breathe but his life was draining from him. I squeezed his neck until I heard it snap. I dropped him on the ground and drank his blood until my stomach was full. Once I was done, I crawled up the wall. After I drank blood, the vampire spirit that possessed my body took over. I ran on top of the building and leaped off. Before I touched the ground, my body transformed into a bat and I took off into the woods.

I landed in a tree and hung upside down. I heard growling seconds later and a beautiful beast with red markings stepped out of the dark. It was a deer a few feet away eating something on the ground. The beast snuck up on the deer and pounced on it—she was a hunter. I knew it was a female beast because of the narrow snout. The beast growled and sank her teeth into the deer's throat. It was a male deer and he was very large but the beast was strong. She snapped its neck and tore into it. After she was finished eating, she shifted back. I caught a glimpse of the markings on her back. Her bottom sat up; it was perfect and round. When she turned around, her breasts were round and her nipples were like dark gems. Chancy was beautiful. She ended our night because she had to hunt. She grabbed her clothes from the bushes and got dressed. I was angry that I couldn't smell her scent the way my beast would've. I no longer cared about getting back to Anubi. I didn't care what Meda's plans were. All I wanted was to become my beast again so that I could mate with Chancy.

Arya

"How is it going, Jose?" I asked the scientist. I walked around my secret lab that was going to make me millions. I knew the pack would've disagreed with what I had planned but it was my life and I wasn't doing anything wrong.

"How many do we have, Laura?" I asked my human friend. She knew what I was and she didn't fear me. I met her a few years ago at a party for Amadi's and Ula's oil line. She was a slim Filipino woman and she wore her hair in a short, boyish cut. She became my best friend and she also helped me with my LOBO line. I learned at a young age that humans were also as sexual as beasts. My real mother was a prostitute for a man named Sosa. He sold her to human men who lived out their wildest fantasies by sleeping with a female beast. Sosa made millions of dollars from his sex ring. I was only ten years old at the time but I understood his angle, sex sells. I didn't want to turn out like him, so instead, I got science involved. We paid a few werewolves to give samples of their DNA to my lab. We mixed their wolf DNA with human DNA. I called it the new age "Wolf Man". It stood up like a man but had a wolf face and gave good pleasure. I wanted to sell the serum to male humans so they could experience what it felt like to be half beast and give great pleasure.

"We have six college students coming in to be testers for the serum," Laura replied to me. After Jose filled up the needles, he stored them inside of a small fridge.

"Maybe we should up the werewolf DNA," Laura suggested.

"No, because the serum might make them permanent shifters. I just want it to be for fantasy purposes. I don't want to create a new breed of 'shifters,'" I replied.

"But what if you do and make even more money? Humans will kill to live forever. You can use this as a 'fountain of youth' drug," she said and I shook my head.

"My pack wouldn't approve of that. I feel bad for doing this but I want my own money. I feel like I'm leeching off of them and their treasure line and skincare line," I replied.

"Look around you, Arya. This lab is from your creations. You are a very smart scientist. Nobody knows what you are capable of but you. Your pack has their own traditions, remember? Where do you fit in with that? You need to start a wealth for the few Indian packs that are left. Give back to them for what Sosa did years ago. You told me how he tore a lot of Indian tribes apart. It's your time to make it right. Pass it down to your pups the same way Goon passed his wealth down to his," she replied. Laura knew everything about me.

"That's different, Laura. Goon comes from ancient royalty. I don't want to force something that isn't there. This is only for pleasure purposes. Nothing more and nothing less. I don't want to create new species. This serum only lasts for an hour and that is it. After an hour, the wolf man will turn back to a human and stay human," I replied and she rolled her eyes.

"Okay, fine. Let's close this down and get out of here. I need a drink," she said. After Laura and I closed down the lab, we headed to a bar. I was thirty years old and didn't have a mate. My body was going into heat and the local werewolves didn't do anything for me. I attracted a lot of males but I didn't find the right one. Maybe because I didn't allow them to bite me or maybe it was because I had someone else in mind.

We sat at the bar and listened to the music. Laura was having fun but I was bored. A few werewolves were in attendance and their scent didn't pique my interest. I paid my tab and said goodbye to Laura. She was promiscuous and so was I. A few nights out of the week after we left the clubs, we attended sex parties. I had sex with more human men than I did werewolves. My life revolved around sex but I couldn't help it. I was taught at an early age from Sosa how to please a man. When I met the pack twenty years ago, they taught me the tradition of the female wolf, but my mind was already damaged. I was saved too late.

When I arrived home, I took my heels off at the door. My mother, Anik, was sitting on the couch waiting for me in the living room.

"Where is Father?" I asked and kissed her cheek.

"He is asleep. Dayo is worried about you and how much you stay away from home. What is going on with you?" she asked. Anik was young when Sosa stole her from her family. She ended up raising me as her own. She wasn't old enough to be my mother but I still called her my mother because she could've left me when she ran away from Sosa but she didn't. She took me with her. Her mate, Dayo, became like my father and over the years he's been very strict. He was also strict with his daughters, Baneet and Chancy. I sat down across from her.

"I need my own life. I come home to this pack and I feel suffocated. Where is my family? I'm the oldest female from the offspring and I should have pups by now," I replied.

"You might just be a late bloomer. You will have pups when you find your mate," she said.

"What if I already did?" I asked. I heard footsteps coming down the stairs. When I looked behind me, it was Kanye. His sweatpants lightly sagged showing off the "V" that formed down to his swinging manhood. His broad chest had unique markings on them. He was a pup but his beast was alluring. Every muscle he possessed was carved into his body. His scent made the desire I had for him form between my legs. I was almost ashamed at how my body gave into his presence because he was still a pup but his scent was too welcoming. Beads of sweat formed on my forehead and wetness poured like a leaking faucet between my legs. I squeezed them together as his eyes gazed over me.

"Ummm, where is your shirt and do you have on boxers?" I asked. His print was visible enough that I could see the prints of the veins he had on his dick through his pants. He was so thick and long and thoughts of him expanding inside of me caused a moan to escape from my lips.

"I'm ready to hunt," he said and headed to the door. I stared at the tribal markings on his back as he left out of the door.

"I need to talk to Kanya about that boy. He isn't a pup anymore," Anik said and stood up.

Indeed, I thought.

"Get some rest, Arya. You look tired," she said and kissed my cheek before she headed up the stairs.

I'm not tired, I'm going into heat and I know just who I need, I thought.

Akea

I sat at the dinner table studying when Chancy came into the house. She went into the fridge and pulled out a pitcher of water. Since our date to the movies, she'd been distant. Maybe it was because she knew I was somewhat into Sarah Baxter. Sarah was intelligent and we had a lot in common—scientifically wise. Chancy was bossy, but she was beautiful and I liked her free spirit. She lived carefree which was something I couldn't do. I just knew I wasn't her speed and we were opposite. I was a warlock and she was a beast. I didn't have much of a social life and she loved to party. *Would I bore her to the point where she'd no longer like me?* I asked myself.

"Oh, hey, Akea," she said when she noticed me.

"Hey, your father was looking for you," I said.

"Oh, I stayed at dance practice late," she said and she hugged me. When she did, I felt her energy and she was lying. I saw images of her and another man, perhaps human. She spent the day with him and he made her laugh. She felt comfortable around him because he appreciated her. She hugged me for five seconds but I was able to read her.

"Are you okay? Your eyes are glowing," she said.

"Yeah, I'm fine. Just a little tired, that's all," I replied.

"Get some rest," she said and walked out of the kitchen. Usually she stuck around me and flirted but she was short with me. My mother came into the kitchen. She sat down next to me and closed my book.

"You studied enough but I want to talk to you about something," she said.

"Okay," I answered.

"I don't like how distant you are from the pack. You have beast blood flowing through your veins, but being a warlock is a gift. You have the ability to use magic," she said.

"Can I show you something? This is just between us, Mother. I don't want Father to know," I said and she nodded her head. I opened the book I was studying and slid it to her. She looked at it.

"What is this?" she asked.

"Old Egyptian drawings. I've been seeing these images in my head and I've been drawing them. It's a spell to become a beast," I said.

"Is this what you've been doing?" she asked and I nodded my head.

"I love you just the way you are. I don't want you to change. If you become a beast, Kanye's beast will challenge you. It's a male thing with brothers that I don't understand, but I don't want to see my sons fighting and ripping each other apart," she said.

"I don't feel like I belong. I feel like a human in a house full of immortals. Witches are closer to humans than any other immortal," I replied.

"That's what makes you unique. But just remember when you force it, it never goes the way you want it to. I'm afraid this spell might ruin you because it's not fate and you are cheating it," she said.

"I understand," I said and closed my book. I thought at least my mother would be on my side about it but she wasn't. No one understood how I felt. I was meant to be a beast and I needed something to bring it out. I had visions of it. After my mother left out of the house to hunt, I grabbed my book and headed to my room.

****

The next day...

"This is cool, isn't it?" Sarah asked me. We were at the museum and I was bored out of mind. Chancy would've added excitement to it in some kind of way, even if it meant her talking about someone. I've been thinking about Chancy a lot, more than I ever did.

"I guess so, but can we leave now? This is boring," I replied.

"But I thought you liked to learn about the mummies," she said.

"I know everything I need to know about them. I will be in the car," I said and walked away from her. She followed me outside to my car and she grabbed my hand.

"What's going on with you? Is it that ghetto trash you went to the movies with? I thought better of you," she said.

"Ghetto trash?" I asked.

"Yes. I see how she acts on campus and if I didn't know any better, I would say she is a whore. She is beneath you. You are on the Dean's List. You are the smartest one on campus and I can't see you settling for her. What goals does she have besides listening to her filthy rap music on campus?" Sarah asked.

"Chancy is not boring but you and I are both boring. Not only are we boring but we are boring together. I don't give a fuck about the Ozone layer nor do I give a damn about the rain forest that's endangered. I've known Chancy since we were babies, so don't talk about her like that!" I said and she gasped.

"That was hurtful, Akea! Take it back!" she yelled and her cheeks turned red.

"Goodbye," I said. I was ready to open my car door but she pulled me away and hugged me.

"I know what you want," she said and her hand slid down to my dick.

Minutes later...

"Ahhhhh, Akea!" Sarah screamed as I pummeled into her. She laid sprawled out in the backseat of my car with sweat beads dripping down her plum-sized breasts.

"It's soooo freakin' big! Fuck me harder!" she screamed and I went deeper. The car rocked back and forth.

His black dick is huge! God, I want him deeper! Fuck me like a little whore! she thought. I pinned her legs up and slammed into her and she screamed out. Her wetness seeped from between her slit and her legs trembled.

"I'm cummmiinnngggggg!" she cried. I pulled out of her and she took me into her mouth. She jerked me off and I pulled her hair. I hit the back of her throat and she gagged but I kept going because I knew I was ready to bust.

"ARRGHHHHH," I groaned when I released inside of her mouth. After we were done, we went to get something to eat. I lied to Chancy because I didn't want to hurt her feelings when I told her that Sarah and I only did it once. Me and Sarah had sex a lot.

I was curious about the guy I saw in Chancy's vision. His gestures were old-fashioned—too old-fashioned. I dropped Sarah off at her dorm after our date and headed home.

****

An hour later...

I knocked on Chancy's door and she yelled out, "Come in!" I opened up her door and she was dressed in a pair of jeans and a tight-fitting shirt. She was applying make-up on her face. I closed the door behind me.

"Do you have a date?" I asked her.

"No, not really. I'm going to hang out with the new boy at school. We are going to the club. Do you want to come?" she asked.

"I don't have nothing to wear," I replied.

"KANYE!" she called out. My brother walked into her room minutes later eating cubes of raw meat. My stomach couldn't tolerate it. Everyone ate bloody meat for dinner but I had to cook a meal for myself. My brother had more muscles than me and even though we were the same size he had more of a warrior figure.

"What's up, loud mouth?" he asked her.

"Help Akea find something to wear for the club tonight," she said and he looked at me and laughed.

"This nigga wants to go to the club? What kind of spell is this, Akea? I know it has to be one if you want to go to the club. I'm warning you, bro, the club we go to doesn't play orchestra and there is a lot of big booties and big titties bouncing. Do you think you can handle that without hand sanitizer?" Kanye asked.

"I can handle it, and just for the record, I don't listen to orchestra, jackass," I said and he chuckled.

"Cool, let me hook you up with something then. My pants might be a little bigger, though. You know we beasts be packing extra weight down there," Kanye teased.

"Stop being a damn dick all of the time and help him find something. Osiris is waiting for us to come," she said.

"Who is that nigga?" Kanye asked.

"A friend," she said and walked out of her bedroom. Kanye looked at me and growled.

"Are you cool with Chancy going out with another male in your face? Bro, come on. Cast some Harry Potter shit on her or something," he said.

"How do you know what I have planned, brother?" I asked and he smirked.

"I knew you had some beast in you. Follow me and I'll help you out," he said. I went into Kanye's room and he headed into his walk-in closet. He pressed a button on the wall and his clothes started moving on the rack.

"You really have one of these?" I asked.

"Yeah, I don't like to pick out clothes," he replied. He let the button go and grabbed a pair of pants off the rack. He grabbed a shirt and grabbed a pair of Jordan's. He gave them to me.

"I was looking for something I didn't wear yet, and, nigga, relax your shoulders. You are always uptight, just be you," he said. It was probably the only real conversation me and my brother had in a long time. I started to regret the distance I put up between us.

"I'm riding with you?" I asked. Kanye had a sports car that didn't hit the show room yet and it received a lot of attention around town. I wanted to know how fast it really was.

"Yeah, you can, but my choice of music," he joked. I left out of his room and went to my room to shower. After I got dressed, we all headed out.

****

"SLOW DOWN!" I yelled out. Kanye was going so fast my stomach was turning. I was ready to get sick. The car lifted up off the ground and froze.

"Nigga, what are you doing?" he asked me and Zaan laughed.

"I stopped the car. I'm ready to be sick!" I said. I opened up the door and threw up.

"He has a virgin stomach," Zaan said.

"What do you do when a female is taking you on a drive of your life?" Zaan asked me. I shut the door and the car dropped onto the road.

"Let me know when you are ready to use that magic stuff. You almost fucked my engine up," Kanye fussed before he sped off.

"I'm used to doing the speed limit," I said and Kanye laughed.

"Bro is going to teach you how to handle horse power. By the time the weekend is over, you are going to ask Father for one of these," he said and went faster. I closed my eyes and Zaan was smoking weed. He passed it to me from the backseat.

"Smoke this and calm your nerves, damn," he said. I took the weed from him and smoked it. I coughed and Kanye patted my back. It felt like my spine was going to crack in half. I felt pain more than them even though I was a fast healer. If I cut myself, it would close up in a few seconds. After five puffs, I got used to the blunt.

When we pulled up to the club, there was a crowd. The loud rap music poured into the parking lot.

"Drink this," Kanye said and passed it to me. When I took a sip of the liquid in the bottle, my chest tightened but I felt good.

"What is this?" I asked.

"Old Egyptian rum," he replied. We got out of the car and headed to the club. I followed Kanye and Zaan and we walked in without waiting in line.

"Our section is upstairs," Kanye said. Once we got upstairs, I was relaxed. I was more relaxed than I had ever been. I had an erection and it stuck against my leg.

"Bro, what was in that liquor?" I asked Kanye.

"You need some pussy, that's all. When you leave the club, take a human with you," he replied. He handed me another blunt and told me to keep it. I smoked and I drank but my mood changed when Chancy walked upstairs with Baneet, Monifa, and the guy from her vision.

"That's the nigga I almost ran into yesterday. I think he is from Africa," Kanye said.

"He is from Anubi," I said and Zaan spit his drink out.

"I thought Anubi's king and Goon made a deal that the two worlds would be separate? I thought no one from Anubi was allowed to come back to Earth because of something that happened twenty years ago?" Zaan asked.

"How do you know he is from Anubi? I thought his accent was a little different, almost old. He speaks like our grandmother, Naobi, but I didn't think of that," Kanye said.

"I saw his face in my vision. I don't know his purpose on Earth but he is from Anubi," I replied.

"He doesn't have a scent like a beast. Everyone in Anubi are werewolves," Kanye said.

"That's what I'm confused about," I replied. They joined our section. The stranger sat down next to Chancy and his eyes darted to me. He almost resembled me and my brother with little traits of our father. The only difference was that his complexion was the color of Midnight.

"Everyone, this is Osiris. Osiris, this is the rest of the crew. The twins are Kanye and Akea and that's Zaan," Chancy said. He bowed his head down which was another old-fashioned gesture.

I can't read his thoughts! Kanye said.

Neither can I! I replied.

He isn't human and he isn't a beast. We can read all humans thoughts. If he was a witch, we'd still be able to read his thoughts. He is a different immortal, Kanye said.

"Let's dance, Kanye," Monifa said.

"I don't dance," he said and she rolled her eyes at him.

You and Monifa mated?

Damn, you must've read her thoughts. I marked her and you'd better not tell our parents. I mean it, bro. I'll chew up your homework so you can go to school and say, "My dog ate my homework." Professors hate that shit, he said. I wondered how he knew that. I imagined Kanye telling his professor that.

Does Monifa know the bartender that's serving this section is someone you went to bed with? I asked Kanye and he choked on his weed smoke. The bartender walked out of the section and tripped on her way leaving out. Monifa laughed and Baneet laughed with her. They must've heard the same thoughts from the bartender about Kanye and her night in the bathroom downstairs. The bartender got up and scurried off. Osiris's eyes were glued to Chancy's thighs. He gently touched her leg and a small bolt of fire burned his fingertips. Osiris had a scowl on his face and a red glare flashed through his eyes. *Definitely immortal,* I thought.

I need to talk to you by the bathrooms! I said to Chancy.

Okay, she answered. I stood up and she walked over to me. I grabbed her hand and walked out of the section and to the hall with the sign "Restrooms" above it.

"What's going on? Is everything okay?" she asked.

"Osiris is an immortal and he is not a beast nor warlock. What is he and what purpose does he have hanging around our pack? He knows what you are, he knows what we all are," I said.

"Are you jealous, Akea? Sarah Baxter isn't fucking you on lunch break anymore? I was in the girl's bathroom with her earlier and I read all of her dirty little thoughts. You told me it only happened once. You are not interested in me, and on top of it all, you lied to me," she said. She kept rambling until I pulled her into me and kissed her. My hands squeezed her bottom and my tongue slid into her mouth. My erection was pressed against her leg and she moaned. We disappeared and reappeared inside of the cleaning closet inside of the club.

"UMMMMM, AKEA!" she screamed out when I began to suck on her neck. My hand slid up her skirt and she gasped. She was dripping on my fingers. She growled and her nails shredded my shirt. I felt scratches going across my chest and her teeth pierced through my shoulder. Pre-cum dripped from the tip of my dick. Even female wolves' bites had an impact. She pulled away from me.

"We need to head back," she said and fixed her clothes. The scratches on my chest closed and my shirt went back to the way it was.

"I got a little bit out of hand, sorry about that. You look beautiful tonight," I replied and smiled.

"You look good enough to bite but don't think I don't notice your liquid courage," she flirted. I opened up the closet door and Osiris was standing in front of it.

"Pardon me for interrupting, but I just wanted to say goodbye before I go back to my sanctuary," he said.

"I'm sorry I left you up there. I will see you in school Monday," Chancy replied. He grabbed her hand and kissed it.

"Most certainly," he replied. A red glare flashed through his eyes and his teeth sharpened when he looked at me. He smirked at me and walked away.

"I'm going to find out what type of immortal he is," I said.

"Osiris is harmless. But let's not waste the night away. Let's dance," she said.

"I don't know how to dance," I replied.

"You don't have to. Just follow my lead," she said and grabbed my hand. The rest of the night I had fun with the pack, the pack that I was a part of. Nothing else mattered to me at that point and Chancy was fresh air. I'd known her all of my life; we all lived together since birth but something spiritual was blossoming between us.

****

"Where are you going?" I asked Chancy. She was running through the dark woods wearing a long, white dress. The dress flared and blew behind her as she ran. Her feet floated above the ground in the woods.

"Wait up!" I called after her as I chased her. She giggled and stopped running. She turned around and stared at me.

"If you want me, Akea, you have to chase me. Promise me you'll always chase me," she said. The moon turned red and blood dripped from her red eyes.

"I promise," I said and reached out to her. She pulled me closer to her and I hugged her. She whispered in my ear.

"It's too late," she said and bit my neck. Her teeth punctured through my flesh like needles. The dark cloud covered the moon and I felt my life slipping from me. She pushed me down on the ground. I wrapped my hands around my neck to keep from bleeding. Before my eyes closed, a bat flew and landed on her shoulder. It stared at me with eyes the same color as blood. It disappeared and Osiris was standing behind her. She kissed him and he smirked at me...

"Akea! Akea! Wake up!" someone screamed. When I opened my eyes, Amadi's mate, Ula, was standing over me. I looked around and I was lying on the kitchen floor. My head was pounding and my mouth was dry.

"You blacked out," she said. I slowly stood up and held my head.

"I've been having weird dreams lately. I can't connect them," I replied.

"Your warlock is becoming stronger. You are able to predict the future," she said. Ula was a witch created from a demon but she fell in love. The love she had for Amadi warmed her cold heart.

"More like nightmares. Do you know the meaning of Vampire Bats?" I asked.

"In Egyptian history, vampire bats were a symbol of the vampire God. He was the only god in his village and people feared him. The villagers sat him out in the sunlight and watched his body turn to ashes after they starved him from blood. His spirit lives through bats. I heard that the bat with the red eyes is the one that possess his spirit and if it bites, his spirit will be transferred to the body he's bitten. But I don't know how true that is because I've never met a vampire," she said and laughed.

"Can this stay between me and you?" I asked.

"I won't tell a soul," she said before she walked out of the kitchen. I didn't want my father to know that a vampire came from his world because I didn't want him to go back to Anubi. I didn't want the pack to defeat an immortal without knowing what they were up against. I had to figure it out myself.

Kanye

I stood under the cold water and growled as I watched a new body marking form on my arms. It was painful and my body was in mid-shift. I punched a hole in the wall and the black ink moved underneath my skin like fire. I howled and my father burst through the door.

"What's going on, Kanye? Is everything okay?" he asked.

"It hurts, Father," I replied. He looked at the marking on my arm and stepped back.

"This can't be. You are too young to mate," he said.

"What?" I asked. He handed me a towel and I stepped out of the shower. My father was taller than me by a few inches. He leaned against the sink and crossed his arms.

"The spiritual gods stamped you. I knew it was going to happen but you are still a pup, Kanye. This shit can't be true. Got damn it!" he shouted and his eyes turned ice blue.

"You ain't ready to become a father. I can't even get you to go to school on time. You smoke weed all day and you are selfish," he said.

"I don't want to have pups. What the fuck? Why can't you teleport and go visit the gods or something? Tell them I'm not ready for this bullshit," I fussed.

"When I met Kanya, I was the same way, but that feeling will go away. You can't control it. I tried to fight it but she gave me two sons that carry my blood. It's the best feeling but I just don't want you to feel it right now. The gods must know you are not responsible," he said.

"Very funny, Pops," I said and left the bathroom. I sat on the bed and stared at my arms. He walked out of the bathroom and joined me.

"When a pup is old enough to mate, the pup's mother's body will naturally crave another pup," he said.

"What?" I asked.

"Your mother will go into heat soon," he replied.

"The gods are some freaky people. All they want us to do is fuck and mate. I wonder if they actually watch us," I said and he chuckled.

"Watch your mouth, son," he said and punched me in the shoulder. I slid into my headboard and it cracked in half. My father laughed out loud. It was how our beasts bonded. At times we made each other bleed and my mother would throw a huge fit but we always ignored it. He shifted and his huge black beast stood in the middle of my bedroom floor, growling. I shifted into my beast and crouched down. He was testing my strength. I charged into him and our beasts went sailing through the window. We rolled down a hill and crashed into a tree. The impact caused the tree to snap in half. Our bodies were like bricks. My father bit my neck and I kicked him off with my hind legs. He leaped into the air and landed on my back. His teeth sank into my neck and I howled. I rolled him over and bit his shoulder. Our beasts went at it; we knocked over trees and blood leaked from our wounds.

"STOP IT! GOT DAMN IT! CUT IT OUT!" my mother screamed. She blew a whistle and it made my ears ring. My father howled before he shifted back to his human form.

"Damn it, Kanya. I keep telling you that I don't like that dog whistle!" he growled and her eyes turned gold and her teeth sharpened.

"You can't play with him like that, Goon! He is bleeding everywhere! You two drive me fucking nuts. Look at the window. We just got a new one put in. Look at my flowers you two ruined. Stop acting like animals," she said. I shifted back and my wounds started to close. I covered my dick with my hands.

"We are animals," I replied and my father chuckled.

"Come on, baby, we are having fun," he said. She was ready to curse but her mouth closed and it couldn't open.

"Peaceful already, beautiful," my father said.

"Did you have to use magic on her, Father?" I asked him.

"Is that a challenge?" he asked me wanting to wrestle again. My mother picked up a shovel and threw it at my father. She tried to talk but she mumbled instead.

"I guess she is really pissed off. Now I'm definitely not unmuting her," he said.

"I can't hear you, beautiful? What was that?" he asked her. She shifted into a golden jackal and chased him into the woods. I heard growling and howling. My parents still acted like teenagers sometimes.

****

Hours later...

"I want to show you something," Monifa said. I was riding in the passenger seat of her car. She woke me up from a nap to come out with her. She pulled up in front of a new building with luxury condos. She got out of the car and I followed behind her.

"I'll be dead by the time you show me what you have to show me," I said growing impatient.

"Shut up, jackass, and follow me," she spat. A few minutes later, we were walking inside of an empty loft with huge floor-to-ceiling windows.

"What do you think?" she asked.

"It's pretty decent but quite small. My bedroom is bigger than this," I replied and she rolled her eyes.

"It doesn't matter. It will be our new home," she said.

"And you decided this without me? We were hating each other a few weeks ago and now we are living together?" I asked.

"I'm not a stranger. We've been around each other since pups and been living together. It's just that this time we will be alone," she replied. Her heels clicked across the floor and her hips swayed side-to-side.

Down boy! I thought to myself because I wanted to enter her.

"I don't know about this," I said and she looked at me with glowing eyes.

"We are going to be having pups and we need our own space," she replied. My cell phone rang and it was someone I met at the Underground club. The Underground club was for werewolves. Her name was Ebony and she was from a pack that migrated from Alaska.

"Busy beast," she said.

"I didn't answer for her."

"So, I have the perfect gown for when we mate. I want to do it right," she said. I forgot how mating and weddings were almost the same. Both ceremonies meant "for life."

"You are really serious about this," I said. I was scared but I couldn't show it. Beasts were not supposed to show fear because it was a sign of being weak.

"Yes, and I'm scared, but I'm naturally prepared for it. You are just stubborn and don't want to realize that this is our destiny," she said.

"I realize it. I can't miss it because it's branded into our skin but I'm being forced to have pups. I don't want pups," I replied.

"Okay, fine," she said. She grabbed her purse off the counter in the kitchen and stormed off to the door.

"Wait, I didn't mean it that way," I called out to her but the door slammed after she walked out. I walked out behind her and she was speed-walking.

"Wait, Monifa!" I called out to her. She walked to her car and opened the driver's side door. I closed the door and she turned around with a scowl on her face.

"What is it?" she asked.

"Why are you sweating like that?" I asked.

"I don't feel good. I need to get home," she said. I smelled her arousal and I knew it was almost time. She was in beginning stages of going into heat. She got in the passenger's seat and I drove home.

****

Two days later...

Monifa locked herself up inside of her room until it was time for school. When I saw her on campus, she walked the other way. She was ignoring me because she was embarrassed. She thought I was rejecting her.

"Excuse me, can you tell me how to get to the cafeteria?" someone asked. When I turned around, it was a girl I'd never seen before. She had long, thick hair with skin the color of butterscotch. She had a few tattoos on her arms and her scent was enticing.

"It's in the 'C' building. Walk behind this one and you will see it," I said.

"Okay, thank you. I'm Fanita by the way. What is your name?" she asked.

"Kanye, but I gotta go," I said and walked off. She was a female werewolf and they were all coming to me because of my scent. My scent was stronger because I was ready to mate and the females that were about to go into heat, wanted my wolf serum. It was hard turning down their arousal.

****

Before my next class started, I headed to the bathroom down the hall from it. After I finished using the bathroom, the door opened. I washed my hands and didn't pay attention to who came in. When I looked up, Osiris was looking at me.

"Nigga, what the fuck do you want?" I asked him.

"I thought you was Akea," he said.

"What do you want with my brother?" I asked.

"How many jewels will it take for me to have Chancy?" he said.

"Nigga, are you serious? Look around you. This ain't Anubi," I spat.

"I don't know what that is," he answered.

"You think I don't know what my people sound like? You came into the bathroom asking to buy someone with jewels. That shit happened before Christ. Now, cut the bullshit and tell me who you are or else I will bite your head off," I said and his eyes turned red.

"I'm the son of Baki and Jesula," he answered.

"The king and queen of Anubi?" I asked.

"I'm prince Osiris and our fathers are brothers. I came to Earth because I am banned from Anubi. I killed one of the warriors and instead of my father punishing me, he sent me here. My mother is a witch and she took my beast from me as punishment. That is the truth," he said.

"You want to fuck your cousin's girl and buy her with some jewels? Nigga, you need to take your ancient ass home," I said and walked out of his face.

"I want to meet my uncle," he called out.

"Excuse me?" I asked.

"I want to meet your father. I heard good stories about him. I admire him as the beast god. The only beast who can change into ancient form. Ancient form is a gift given from the gods. I want to be him some day," he said.

"You cannot meet my father and you will not step foot on our territory. You are still considered another beast from another pack," I replied and he shrugged his shoulders.

"See you soon," he said and left the bathroom. When I left out, Yardi and a few of his football friends were standing in the hallway.

"Punk," he said when I walked passed him. I turned around and walked up on him.

"Do you got something you want to say to me?" I asked.

"You can't keep her for too long," he said and his friends chuckled.

"I have her for life. You will get the picture once you see her pushing a stroller with our twins inside of it," I replied and he bit his bottom lip. He pointed his finger in my face.

"I will kick your ass!" he yelled and I laughed.

"The day you turn into a beast might be the day you can challenge me, nigga, and I put that on God," I spat and walked away.

That muthafucka got one more time threatening me and I will eat him alive, I thought.

******

"Hey, big head," Arya said when she came into the kitchen. I just got back in from hunting and I was drinking a pitcher of water. Arya was the oldest out of all of us.

"What's good witchu?" I asked.

"Are you busy tonight? I need to go to this party but I don't have anyone to escort me. Everyone else seems to be busy," she said.

"What kind of party?" I asked.

"I was invited to this event held by *Fair Essence* magazine. I wanted to advertise Amadi's oil and Beastly Treasures' new jewelry line. The charm bracelet with the faces of kings and queens that ruled Egypt are going to be a hit. The diamonds in the bracelets are beautiful. You have to see it," she said. Arya was out in the field a lot. I rarely saw her in the house and when she was home, she was glued to the computer.

"How do I have to dress?" I asked.

"Suit, and I know you have plenty. Our limo will be here in three hours so don't be late," she said and walked off. Arya was pretty and she had a set of big brown eyes. Her Indian features were strong. She had high cheekbones, a pointed nose, and thick, black hair that she kept pinned up.

****

Four hours later...

Arya had her hand through my arm as we walked around the party inside of a colonial-style white mansion. There was a lot of rich people in attendance and Arya fit right in. She talked liked them and even laughed at their corny jokes. She was dressed in a long, black dress that clung to her curves with the back out. She unpinned her hair and thick coals fell down her shoulders. My tuxedo was all-black and I wore my diamond chain necklace with the matching bracelet. I received a lot of compliments on my jewelry. It was a part of the Beastly Treasures line.

"There is a secret event going on downstairs when the party is over. We have passes to it," Arya said.

I sipped on my champagne and stood off to the side while Arya interacted with the humans. When I came into pre-teens, I had the biggest crush on Arya. I used to sneak into the bathroom when she showered. Her scent caused me to have wet dreams and Zaan teased me about it. I grew out of it as the years passed because she was older and more mature. I started thinking about Monifa because she was still giving me the cold shoulder.

Are you still mad at me? I asked Monifa and she didn't respond. I had visions of her taking a bath in my head.

Are you still mad at me? I asked her again and she didn't respond. She heard me but she ignored me.

Fuck you! I said.

Fuck someone else. Better yet, fuck Arya! You two look nice by the way. Matching colors and occasionally staring at her ass when she walks. I can see it all! she yelled.

You are crazy! I wasn't looking at her ass! I replied and she didn't respond.

"You look troubled. Is everything okay?" Arya asked. I didn't want to tell her about Monifa because Arya tells Dayo everything and Dayo would've told Izra to piss him off. Dayo and Izra always fought but my father said it had always been that way.

"I'm fine," I replied.

"You look very handsome tonight by the way. You really have grown into a remarkable beast," she said.

"Appreciate it, you don't look too bad yourself," I replied and she blushed. An hour later, I was buzzed and the majority of the crowd started to leave the big mansion. Fifteen of us were left and we headed downstairs. We walked down a long hall in the cellar and stopped when we came to a big, brown wooden door.

"Okay, ladies and gentlemen. Beyond this door is the key to changing our human mankind," the middle-aged Hispanic man said. He wore a lab coat and his glasses were thick, almost reminded me of magnifying glasses.

"What is this and why are we invited?" I asked Arya.

"I paid for the show. I heard it was something to see but the details were always a secret. I was curious to see what everyone was addicted to at these parties," she said. The door opened and there was a small theatre inside. The red curtains on the stage were closed and candles were lit everywhere. I sat down next to Arya and we waited for the show to begin.

"This better be worth my time. I'm getting hungry," I said and she giggled. The Hispanic man stepped onto the stage with a microphone.

"Ladies and gentlemen, enjoy the show!" he said and hurriedly walked off. The lights in the theatre dimmed and the curtains opened. A black man was tied to a table.

"What and the fuck is this? Slavery is over," I said to Arya.

"Just watch the show," she replied. My blood started to boil and I growled. My father and his pack brothers told me a lot about the slavery days. My father was a slave before he found out who he was. I wanted to attack the man on stage for participating in the show, a show with only two black people in the audience. The Hispanic guy walked over to the man with a long needle. He stuck it inside of the man's neck and he screamed. The Hispanic man hurriedly ran off-stage. Two minutes later, the black man's body started to shake and tremble. He screamed and yelled as his body bubbled. His legs grew longer and so did his arms. Gray strands of stringy hair pierced through his skin. His fingers snapped back and the crunching sound of bones reforming was familiar. He was shifting into something. His face grew out into a snout and his ears grew upwards; it pulled the skin back on his face and specs of blood dripped on the stage. Everyone sat and watched with amazement but I felt my body changing. My beast didn't like being in the presence of another male beast from a different territory.

"Don't do it here," Arya said with her eyes glowing. I growled at her. The beast broke away from the table and he stood up like a man. He was a lab created werewolf.

Real werewolves looked like wolves but just larger in size but the image before me was the same one in the movies. Humans always tampered with originality. A woman walked on stage and she looked familiar. It was Fanita, the woman I met on campus. She wore a silk black robe and she dropped it. Her pussy was shaved bald. Her sex popped out like a peach and I saw the drippings of her sex slide down on her leg. She was aroused and so was my beast. Her scent filled the theatre and it was strong. My head started to spin and I felt myself shifting. Arya grabbed my hand and squeezed it.

Keep him calm, Kanye, Arya said. The wolf man howled and his dick grew from between his legs. Fanita grabbed him and massaged his shaft. He laid her on the table and pushed her legs back and it exposed her sex. His tongue entered her and she screamed. Her nails dug in his back. He came up from between her legs and grabbed her breast with his large hand. He stuck it inside of his mouth and his teeth gently sank into her flesh. Her eyes rolled into the back of her head. He stuffed himself inside of her. She moaned in pleasure and her eyes glowed. Her nipples were hard and sticking up. Another scent mixed in with Fanita's and it was even better. It was coming from next to me. Arya whined and her nipples poked through her dress. By the scent of her arousal, I could tell she was in heat.

I'm in the house with two females in heat? This shit is torture, I thought. Arya started to moan and her skin looked sweaty.

"Touch me," she whispered. She pulled her dress up and slid her wet thong down to her ankles. She opened her legs and my erection grew; it dripped with pre-cum.

"Kanye, touch me!" she said. The beast was ramming himself into Fanita on stage. Arya and I were seated in the back behind the audience.

"I can't," I replied. She grabbed my hand and stuck it between her legs. She was warm—almost hot. She bucked her hips forward on my hand and growled. I squeezed her breast and my teeth expanded. My nails sharpened and it dug into the fabric of her dress. She moaned louder and her body trembled when she came on my hand. She got down on the floor and pulled my dick out of my pants. It swelled and the veins were so thick, it reminded me of pipes. She stroked it and her big eyes glowed; her lips turned black and her hair grew out into a mane. Her long tongue caught the pre-cum that dripped from my large head. She placed her mouth on me and slid me to the back of her throat and I howled. The people in front of us was into the show and my howl fell on deaf ears. I heard the sounds of Monifa's sniffles in my head. She could see everything I did. Spiritually, I belonged to her and even though I was fighting it, I still belonged to her. I pulled myself out of Arya's mouth and fixed my pants. I stood up and hurried out of the theatre. I walked down the hall angry with myself. Arya's heels clicked across the floor.

"Kanye! Wait," she said and caught up to me. She grabbed my hand and turned me around.

"I'm soooo sorry! I'm really sorry! I'm in heat and I couldn't control it. Seeing that show had me so aroused. I'm truly sorry. I'm so embarrassed," she said.

"What the fuck did you bring me to?" I asked her. I grabbed her by the neck and held her up against the wall.

"What did you bring me to? You knew I was developing wolf serum to mate with. You can smell it on me and that's why you brought me here. I will snap your damn throat," I said.

"My beast has been craving you all day and I brought you here because I wanted it to be a date. I wanted to see if your beast could get me aroused as I imagined," she said. I dropped her on the ground.

"You knew they were going to fuck and you set me up," I said. She stood up and dusted herself off.

"I knew you were going to enjoy it like how you enjoyed watching me when you were younger. I've been waiting until your beast came of age. Once a male develops wolf serum, he is full-grown. You are no longer a pup, Kanye," she said.

"What was that back there? Humans turning into beasts from injections is dangerous," I said.

"It's a new line that the elite is working on. It's for pleasure purposes. Every woman, human or immortal, wants a beast in the bedroom. Strong, hard, big, and aggressive. It's like living out your true fantasy. The serum comes from werewolves. The werewolves are selling their blood to the lab. The scientist used their blood mixed with Viagra and it gives you a bedroom beast. It's the new fantasy of the century," she replied.

"Why would a werewolf risk their tradition like this by selling their blood to be tested on? There is not enough money for that," I said.

"Not every werewolf comes from ancient wealth. A lot of young wolves do it, the ones that want to live like humans. Drive the fancy cars, go on shopping sprees and have a lot of cash. It's innocent, Kanye," she said.

"It's dangerous, dumb ass. I should've known you was all beauty and no brains. Do you know that these new fake species of wolves can become a problem? They are a threat to us and need to die," I said.

"They don't have scents and can't be detected, so how will you find one and kill it?" she asked.

"How do we stop it?" I asked.

"I don't know," she spat. The door opened and the audience walked out, fanning themselves. I heard some of their thoughts and most of them couldn't wait to get in their cars to fondle each other. I headed back into the theatre and the beast was on stage eating a raw steak. The Hispanic guy stood and watched him. Fanita stood with her robe on.

"Great show," I said.

"It's over and you can leave like everyone else," the man spat. My eyes turned and he backed away. The beast growled at me and stood up on his feet with meat stuck between his teeth.

"You should be ashamed," I said to Fanita and she stepped back.

"Get out!" the man yelled at me. I leaped into the air and shifted. My large beast knocked him down on the stage and I sank my teeth into his neck. His blood squirted into my mouth as I tore the scientist to shreds. Fanita shifted and attacked me. I tossed her into a rail and her back snapped. She laid on the floor and whimpered. The man wolf ran to me and I tackled him down to the floor. His nails dug into my neck and he bit my snout. I went for his neck and he howled. It picked me up and slammed me. It was strong, very strong, but I wanted it dead. It growled and I bit his arm and slung him off the stage and he went sailing into the chairs. I leaped on him and went for his throat. I shook him down and clamped harder onto his throat. He howled and I yanked away from his neck pulling a chunk out. I could see the floor through his neck while he lay bleeding to death. I walked over to Fanita and she couldn't move.

Please help me, she pleaded. I snapped her neck with my teeth. I crawled up the wall and burst out of the window. I leaped over a few cars and landed in the woods. It took me fifteen minutes to get home on foot. When I got to the house, I crawled up the wall. I pushed Monifa's window in and crawled into her room. The nails from my paws scrapped across her bedroom floor. She sat up and turned the light on. She was naked underneath the sheet. I shifted into human form and headed to her bathroom. I turned the water on in the shower. She followed me into the bathroom.

"The nerve of you coming into my room with her scent on your fingers!" she yelled.

"I didn't mean to do it. It won't happen again," I replied. A force slammed me into the shower and the wall cracked. The water pipe burst and sprayed her bathroom. Her eyes turned pitch black and her teeth sharpened. Her nails grew long and pointy. She smacked me in the face and I felt my skin opening on my cheek. My blood mixed in with the water that was flooded across the floor.

"It was painful to see that, Kanye. It was very painful to see through your eyes the desire you had for her. I have to see her every day because she's in the same pack. Maybe the gods of fate made a mistake because I hate you. I want to cut your dick off and shove it down your throat. Get the hell out of my room before I turn you into a cockroach and then step on you," she seethed. I stood up and smirked. I kissed her fingertips and her forehead.

"We shouldn't be tricked into desire. It should come naturally, and naturally I want you. I was purposely put on the spot tonight and it won't happen again," I said.

Her eyes changed back to their normal color. The bathroom went back to the way it was before the pipe burst. She ran the bath water and waited until it was full. She turned the water off then dipped her finger inside of it. The water turned into milk and honey.

"Witches are always up to something," I said. She pulled me inside of the oval-shaped tub that was big enough for four humans. I laid between her legs and her breasts were pressed against my back. The connection was there and my spirit was meshed with hers. Nothing else mattered to me at that moment. She could lock me up for life and I wouldn't miss anything.

"You feel it, too?" she asked in my ear.

"I felt it when I touched Arya," I replied. She kissed my neck and gently bit me. I growled from the tease she was giving me.

"The moon we mate under is coming in a few weeks. I still need to tell my father about it and about the new home I'm moving into," she said and rubbed my back. She squeezed my shoulders and I almost fell asleep.

"I actually like you like this. You were always bitchy. I will tell Izra about us and the rest of the pack. If you are going to be pregnant, we need to tell them as soon as they wake up in the morning," I replied.

"I saw through your eyes what you did to that beast tonight. Are you worried about that?" she asked.

"If there are a lot of fake beasts roaming around, it will cause mayhem. The injection has Viagra in it and it makes them very aroused. What if someone doesn't want to have sex. Will they force it? I told myself that it wasn't my concern but my beast is threatened by it," I replied.

"I don't trust Arya, Kanye. She's up to something and I can't see her visions the way I can see everyone else's because of our different tribes. She's not connected to the circle of our ancestors," Monifa said.

"I think she's just in heat," I replied.

"I think it's more to her than what she's letting on. She knows about those wolf men. I saw it through your eyes when you were talking to her that she does. She made it seem as if it wasn't a big deal," she replied.

"We will find out," I replied. Afterwards, we showered and dried off. I got into bed with her and pulled her close to me.

"I want to show you something," she said and jumped up. She crawled up the wall and onto the ceiling. She turned her body around and her back was pressed against the ceiling. She spread her legs and my body raised off of the bed. Monifa took full advantage of being a witch. A force pulled me into her and I was rested between her legs. She wrapped her arms around me and I entered her. She gasped and moaned. I didn't care about falling, all I wanted to do was please her. My nails dug into the ceiling and she wrapped her legs around me. I pumped in and out of her and she chanted my name. Her nails scratched me and I felt drops of blood rolling down my back. She almost howled but I covered her mouth. We made love until the next morning.

Monifa

"You are happy this morning," Baneet said to me. We were walking through the woods on our way back home from hunting.

"Kanye and I had a long night," I said and she smiled.

"I thought I heard something," Chancy said.

"It's so amazing. My body burns each time he pushes more of himself inside of me. He makes me promiscuous," I said and Baneet laughed.

"As much as Zaan and I sneak off, you would think we would have that spiritual connection," Baneet said.

"That's because you won't allow him to bite you," Chancy said annoyed. Arya walked into the woods and she was naked. Her perfectly sculpted body was very mature and she had a big butt. Her perky breasts sat up, and when she walked, her hips swayed—seductively.

"Good morning, girls. You all couldn't wait for me?" she asked.

"You were asleep when I came into your room," Baneet said.

"She had a long night last night. Her and Kanye hung out," I said.

"Yes, the party was beautifully decorated. Service was great and the food was awesome. Kanye enjoyed their selection of champagne. We really had a blast," she said.

"You had a blast on his fingers," I spat and her smile turned into a scowl.

"What are you talking about?" Arya asked.

"Nothing important since I made myself clear already," I said and walked away. I grabbed my clothes and got dressed. When I walked into the house, my father was coming downstairs. He could pass for my older brother.

"Hey, Father," I said.

"What's up with my beautiful daughter? I feel like I haven't been seeing you lately," he said.

"I know. I've been busy with school. How was the trip? Did you and Uncle Elle have fun?" I asked him.

"Elle's old ass had fun. I missed my leather chair and big screen TV," he said. I followed him into the kitchen and he grabbed a pitcher of water from the fridge.

"Can I ask you something?"

"Nope," he answered.

"Why?" I asked.

"Every time you ask, 'Can I ask you something? it's always something that upsets me. Remember when you asked me about going to the movies with that human boy, Yarn? I couldn't sleep," he said and I laughed. My father was stubborn and hated when I did anything that wasn't about school. I understood his worries because I was the only child and my mother couldn't give him anymore children. He wanted me to stay his little girl forever.

"His name is Yardi and we broke up," I said and he spit his water out. A growl slipped from his lips.

"You was with that nigga? I thought y'all was just studying but you broke up with him, meaning you was his girlfriend and he put his funky-ass human fingers on you? ADDIKKKAAAAAAA!" he called out. Baneet and Chancy walked into the house and started laughing on their way upstairs. My mother came into the kitchen wearing a hooded cape.

"What in the hell is going on? I keep telling you to stop watching *Sister Act.* Where are you going?" he asked her.

"I'm a Muslim," she said.

"Come again?" he asked.

"I'm a Muslim now. What do you think? Do you like it?" she asked. My parents were the most complicated couple in the house.

"I'm tired, beautiful. I was on a long, boring trip with Elle and I almost lost my beast. Elle has got to be the most boring pack brother I have. I don't understand him. I probably never will," my father fussed.

"Grumpy old man. What did you call me for?" she asked him.

"You didn't tell me Monifa had a human boyfriend," he seethed.

"It's old, and besides, she is grown now. She is not a little girl anymore. Pretty soon, she will be ready to have pups and we can be grandparents," she said.

"I'm the youngest out of all my pack brothers and I will be damned if I'm a grandparent before all of them," he fussed.

"Well, Daddy. That's what I have to talk to you about," I said. Kanye came into the kitchen, shirtless, with a pair of sweatpants on and that bubbly feeling started to form again. I had butterflies and it made me giggle because it tickled. He grabbed a tray of raw meat from out of the fridge. He kissed my mother on the cheek and gave my father some type of handshake that all of the males in the house did.

"I left a little stash for you under your mattress," my father said to Kanye and my mother hit him.

"What? Kanye likes to smoke and so do I. The boy is a man now and he can smoke a little herb," my father said.

"Kanye is man but Monifa is a little girl and they are the same age? What sense does that make?" my mother asked him. Kanye chewed the meat while my parents argued. He winked at me and a little drop of blood dripped from his lip. His pretty, white sharp teeth chewed through the thick chunk of meat. I wanted to lick his full lips.

"Father, I need to tell you something!" I yelled over him and my mother.

"Okay, what is it?" he asked. Kanye dropped the tray of meat because he knew what I wanted to tell them. I grabbed Kanye's hand.

"Me and Monifa are soulmates. I'm going to mate with her for life," Kanye whispered.

"What in the fuck did you just say? I should've stayed on that camel's back in Egypt with Elle's old ass," my father said.

"Calm down, Izra," my mother said. My father started to sweat and his eyes began to change. He banged his fist on the counter and it caved in. He pointed at my mother.

"Is this another spell of yours? Are you still mad because I went on the trip and forgot to tell you? What is this?" he asked. Kanye turned me around and ripped my shirt open, exposing my back.

"She has your marking? She is ready to mate and have pups?" my father asked but Kanye didn't respond. I turned around and his face was starting to change. He slammed his fist into the fridge and put a dent in it.

"We can't control fate," Kanye said. My father burst out of his clothes and shifted into his beast. His sharp teeth clamped down on Kanye's shoulder and I screamed. Kanye turned into his beast and slammed my father onto the kitchen table. They were rolling around the kitchen, biting each other, leaving blood everywhere. An electrical bolt shot out of my hand and separated them. Kanye paced back and forth licking his teeth with a scowl on his face. His ears pointed back and his upper body crouched down. He growled then howled at my father, challenging him. My father tried to charge into him but my mother put a shield over Kanye.

"ENOUGH!" she yelled. Goon came into the kitchen and looked around. He saw Kanye's shoulder dripping with blood. When Goon shifted, his beast charged into my father. They went to each other's throats. It was the worse fight I'd seen within the pack. My father bit Goon's snout and Kanye jumped on him. I used a force to knock Kanye off and I blocked him with a shield. He charged into the bubble but he couldn't get through. Kanye was supposed to protect his father but it was my father he wanted to hurt. I couldn't let him do it. My mother tried to break them up but Goon was too strong. He was a beast and a warlock, he had the ability to block my mother's magic. The rest of the pack ran into the kitchen and pulled them apart. Everyone was in beast form except for me and my mother. The kitchen was ruined because of Goon and my father. When they were pulled apart, my father leaped over the rest of the pack and attacked Kanye when I unshielded him. Kanye and my father went at it and ended up going through a wall. Goon charged into my father and slammed him. My father was a fighter and he wasn't backing down. Ula made a noise and it rang through all of our ears. I fell down to the floor and screamed. Everyone shifted back and laid sprawled out on the floor, holding their ears.

"THAT IS ENOUGH!" she screamed. My mother put clothes on everybody because everyone was naked.

"Son of a bitch!" my father said to Goon.

"You attacked my son, Izra? You attacked my goddamn son? If you have any problems with my pups, you come to me. You don't attack my son!" Goon yelled at him.

"Your son is trying to fuck my daughter! She is still a pup!" my father yelled. I ran out of the house and my mother called after me. I ran until I couldn't run anymore and burst into tears. I felt like I had to choose my father or Kanye, but I couldn't stay away from Kanye because we were connected to each other.

* * * * * * * * *

Three days later...

I sat in my condo and looked out of the window. The rain was pouring down and I blocked everyone from my thoughts. It took me a while to master it, but I decorated the place with magic. I laid across the cheetah fur couch and thought about Kanye. I knew everyone was concerned about me but I needed my space. I always wanted my space. There were too many families living in that house, but even with the large number of people, there was still room for more. I fell asleep.

I heard someone walking around in my home. I sat up and looked around and blue eyes stared at me from the corner of the room.

"It's funny watching you sleep. You sound like a gorilla when you snore," Kanye said.

"What are you doing here?" I asked. He walked over to me and sat down beside me.

"I wanted you to cool off so I stayed away for a few days. I knew where you went off to and so did your mother," he said. He took off his T-shirt and threw it on the floor. He laid down behind me and wrapped his arm around me. I inhaled the smell of his cologne mixed in with his natural scent.

"Izra means a lot to me and it crushed me that I attacked him. Me and him might not ever get along again. It crushed my father, too, that he attacked Izra. This thing with us is breaking the pack apart," he said.

"We can ignore fate if we really try," I said.

"I don't want to. We can stay here. I got everything I need downstairs in my car. I was going to shift and carry all of that shit on my back through the window, but I'll scare a lot of muthafuckas," he said. I turned to face him.

"Are you serious?" I asked.

"Yeah, it's too many niggas in that house," he said and I laughed. In just that short period of time, I was feeling peaceful again. Anytime Kanye was near, I felt whole.

"Let's drink some milk with honey," I said. It was my favorite snack. My mother loved it and she always had it when she was pregnant with me.

"I'm thirsty but not for that," he growled. His hand slid into my boy shorts. He pulled his fingers from between my legs and, like always, I was dripping. He licked my essence from off his fingers and his eyes changed. He ripped my panties off and picked me up and over his head—he was strong like an Ox.

"What are you doing?" I asked. He held me above his head like he was lifting weights. He placed me on top of his tongue and I moaned out. He lifted me up and down on his face with my essence dripping down to the back of his throat. It was insanely naughty but I was passed turned on. His tongue went in and out of me like a dick and my pussy clenched. I rubbed my clit as my nipples hardened. My heartbeat raced and my skin felt clammy— really clammy. He slurped on my nectar and I lost control when his sharp teeth pierced through the lips of my vagina. I moaned and the glass vase shattered on the kitchen island. Cracks started forming in the windows. My energy filled the room. He slid his pants down and freed himself. He pulled me down on his massive dick and my stomach cramped. With each day that passed, my body craved for pleasure even more. It craved pleasure on levels that I couldn't handle and mating was going to be the cure.

****

The next day...

"Can I talk to you? It will only be for a second," Yardi said to me. He was standing outside of the Café next to the campus. I always ordered a cup of hot milk with honey. I drank it every morning like it was coffee.

"Make it quick because I have another class in thirty minutes," I replied. I sat down on the bench and he sat down next to me. He caressed my face with sadness in his eyes.

"I miss you," he said.

"We had a good relationship but now I'm with Kanye," I said.

"I heard he was your cousin. His father and your father are brothers right?" he asked.

What a dummy, I thought.

"That is why you go to the source before you start listening to stupid shit. My father and his father are not blood brothers, moron. My father has close friends that he grew up with that he refers to as brothers," I spat.

"I heard your father still looks the same from twenty years ago," he said.

"Amadi's oil does the body good. Maybe you should try it because your face is going to crack when I walk away from you," I said when I stood up. I grabbed my backpack.

"Black don't crack. My father still looks young and acts young. That's a human blessing, right?" I asked.

"No need to be upset. That's the word around campus," he replied.

"Goodbye Yardi," I said and walked away.

What the fuck does he want, now? Kanye asked.

Jealous? I asked.

Hell no! he said and I chuckled. I knew he was jealous because most male wolves were. After my classes were over, I headed to my car. My father was standing by my car and I stopped in my tracks. I knew sooner or later he was going to catch up to me. I tried to figure out his mood but his expression was blank. I tried to read his thoughts but he wasn't thinking anything. He was shutting everyone out which he did a lot when he was angry. I walked over to him.

"Hi, Father," I said.

"I heard you are living out on your own," he said.

"It's the only way Kanye and I can have our privacy," I replied and he growled.

"This shit is tough. I fought my closest brother. I attacked his son and you moved out. I'm trying to deal with this fate shit but it's hard," he said.

"I'm not a little girl anymore and I can't help who I am. You and mother created me. I'm a child of two immortals. I'm part beast, which is from you. I cannot control the urges I have because of my beast, and going into heat is one of them. How can you not accept something that is from you, Father?" I asked.

"I understand fate but I can't help but to be pissed off. I don't have a choice because when the gods are ready for new life to be created it happens. I guess the positive side of it is that I've known Kanye since he was a pup. I would've killed him if he was from a different pack," he said and I laughed.

"I would've helped you," I replied and I hugged him. When I hugged my father, I saw his vision and I felt his sadness. He wasn't angry, he was sad because my mother couldn't give him another baby and he wanted more. I pulled away from him.

"Being a grandparent is like being a parent. My pups will be a part of you and you will watch them grow up," I said and he smirked. Kanye walked out of school and headed toward my car. When he saw my father, he froze.

"Bring your ass over here, boy," he said to Kanye. Kanye walked over to us.

"What's up? There's too many humans around, so if you came to fight, the woods are right across the parking lot," he said and my father laughed.

"I'm still trying to heal from your bite mark. Uncle Izra is done fucking with you and your father. I almost forgot about his ancient beast," he said. Kanye hugged him and squeezed him. I heard my father's bone crack.

"I can't breathe," he said.

"Oh, my bad," Kanye said and patted his shoulder and my father winced. Kanye was very strong and, at times, he didn't realize it.

"I need to get going. I've got to drop a few things off at Beastly Treasures," my father said. He got on his motorcycle and a few college girls waved at him and tried to get his attention.

"He still got it," I said.

****

Later on that night...

I was in the laundry room putting clothes inside of the washer when I heard a loud thump from upstairs. Kanye came inside the laundry room.

"Did you hear that?" he asked. I heard another loud thump followed by a scream. Kanye sniffed the air.

"I smell blood," he said and sniffed the air again. His eyes turned blue. A woman screamed louder and I heard another bang. Kanye rushed out of the house and I followed him. He went to the door where the screams were coming from. He kicked the door down and I walked in behind him. The smell of blood was stronger and my body started to shift. A couch flew across the room and a naked white woman with red hair was in the corner, screaming. She looked like she was in her mid-twenties. A big, grey wolf stepped in front of us from around the corner of the living room. He stood up like a man. He reminded me of the image "Hollywood" portrayed in movies about werewolves when only ancient beasts like Goon stood up like a man. The werewolf towered over Kanye. Kanye shifted and charged into him. I ran to the woman who was balled up in a fetal position in the corner of the living room.

"Something is wrong with him. We were ready to be intimate and he just turned into one of those!" she cried. It was the beast Kanye warned me about. When I turned around, the beast grabbed Kanye by his neck and I shifted. After I shifted, I charged into the beast. I jumped on his back and my teeth sank into its neck. He howled when Kanye's sharp teeth bit his fingers off. After the beast collapsed, we tore into him. The woman screamed louder. Blood flew on the walls and Kanye ripped his stomach open. The beast stopped breathing and I backed away. It was my first time killing a beast. I shifted back and turned the beast into a pile of ash from the electricity that came from my eyes. I smelled fresh urine and when I turned around, it was flowing down the floor and toward me. It came from the stranger; she was more terrified of Kanye's oversized beast more than she was of the wolf man.

"He's not going to hurt you. What did you use?" I asked her. She slowly stood up and walked passed Kanye. Kanye growled at her and she jumped up. She was trembling and she held her breath—she was scared to breathe.

"It's okay. He naturally growls," I said.

We have to kill her. We live downstairs from her. What if she tells the police that we killed her boyfriend? Even if they don't believe her story, we still killed her boyfriend," Kanye said.

I have a plan.

The woman went to her purse in the corner of her room and picked up a box with the words "LOBO" written on the box. *Lobo* meant "Wolf" in the Filipino language.

"Where did you get this?" I asked and she started crying.

"Lyle was a tester for the lab. It was his birthday and he asked me if I could be intimate with his beast. He said it would bring great pleasure. I let him talk me into it but something was wrong and I didn't want to do it anymore. He tried to rape me when he turned into it. He was a monster," she said.

Just like I predicted. The beast will become so aroused that they won't understand the word "No" and an aroused beast becomes aggressive. I need to find the lab, because if we don't, our true identity will be exposed to mankind, Kanye said.

"Where is the lab?" I asked.

"I don't know but it's in the city. I never saw it but when he goes to get this stuff, he is only gone for an hour," she cried. "Are you going to kill me? I promise I won't say a word about what I saw," she said.

Don't believe her, she's lying. I can hear her thoughts, he said. She looked at me and backed away because my eyes turned black. She fell over the couch and I walked closer to her. I blew on her and her body turned to glass then she shattered. Pieces of her scattered across the floor. I heard someone coming from down the hall. I listened closely and it was the police.

"The noise was coming from that apartment," someone said. I got on Kanye's back and he ran and burst through the window. The glass cut my face but it immediately closed.

BOOM!

He landed on a truck and the windows shattered like dust. He ran into the woods and leaped up a tree. We stayed in the woods until the coast was clear.

Arya

I snuck into the lab to delete all of my files inside of the computers. Everything traced back to Jose just in case something went down because my name wasn't on anything anymore. After Kanye snapped on one of the scientists and my project at the show, I closed down the lab and forgot to delete all of my files.

"Are you really trying to let this all go?" Laura asked me while I sat at my desk.

"Kanye is on to us! If I was a wolf from Anubi, they would've been figured me out," I fussed.

"How does that work, exactly? They can't see your visions because you have different roots?" she asked.

"Exactly! They can only hear my thoughts when I'm around but they don't have a connection to me," I spat. I erased all of my information from the computer.

"This is a genius idea and it's going to waste," she fussed.

"Something is wrong with the LOBO brand! I've received a few messages about it this morning. The humans are becoming aggressive when they turn into the beast. It wasn't supposed to get out of hand like this. Where did I go wrong with it?" I asked. Laura sat down next to me and rubbed her temples.

"I have a confession," she said and I looked at her.

"I told Jose that you wanted to up the dosage of the wolf DNA. I didn't think it was going to get out of hand. We tested it on a student and he went bizarre inside the lab. I told Jose to destroy it but I don't think he did. I think he is selling it on the streets," she said.

"BITCH! How could you do this to me?" I asked and shoved her into a desk. The desk flipped over and the back of her head bled. She sat up and touched the wound. Blood was on her fingertips. She smirked at me and the blood disappeared.

"Big mistake, bitch!" she said and all the tables flew across the room. The lights in the ceilings exploded and a piece of glass flew into my cheek. I growled at her and she laughed.

"Oh, Arya. Things are not always what they seem," she said and her image disappeared. A thick, curvy woman stood in front of me with white locks and black eyes. She was dressed in a long, gold wraparound dress and she had a diamond in the middle of her forehead. Her nails were long and sharp and they were the color of blood. She held her hand out and a black cloud encircled her palm.

"My name is Meda. Your real friend, Laura, has been dead for a few months now. I stole her identity to get close to you," she said. The black cloud floated from her palm and into my mouth. I gasped for air and fell onto the floor. She kneeled down beside me.

"Don't worry. It's just something to paralyze you because you talk too much and I want you to hear me. I used you for your brain. I've been watching Goon and his pack over the years and I knew you could help me with what I needed. I knew Naobi and Goon couldn't see your visions and that's why I needed you. I knew you had a gift to create what I was looking for. Why do you think I helped you with the idea? I could've created my own beast but it would've taken many years. You did it in three months. But I can't let you destroy them because I have a plan for them. I want them to kill Goon and destroy the rest of his pack," she said and tears fell from my eyes. She wiped them away and poked her lip out.

"Poor baby, you don't belong with them anyway. You are a jezebel, just like your mother was," she said and stood up. A bat flew into the lab and it turned into a young man. He was strikingly handsome and resembled Goon and his sons—a lot.

"This is my nephew, Osiris. We will take it from here," she said and walked away. I laid on the floor and I couldn't move or talk. I watched him bite his arm and the blood dripped from his arm inside the tubes that sat on the table.

"I know you are wondering what I am doing. I'm giving your LOBO brand blood from a vampire. They will feed on your humans on Earth, turning them into bloodsucking beasts. This is what I've always wanted. And I won't stop until I get my revenge," she said. Her nephew looked at me with saddened eyes but I could tell that something dark was hidden inside him. His eyes turned red and I remembered when Kanya said that red eyes meant "Demon." Osiris put all of the tubes inside of a backpack.

"You will not have any memory of this. Not me or the LOBO brand. All of the information you have from this lab is gone from your memory. I will see you soon, best friend," was all I heard before my world went black...

****

I opened my eyes and the sun beamed in my face. I looked around and I was inside of Laura's apartment. I sat up and my head was throbbing.

"Girl, we had a blast last night," Laura said and handed me a cup of coffee. My stomach was turning and my mouth was dry.

"I must've had too much to drink. I don't remember anything," I said.

"Well, I do. In a few hours, you have to be at Amadi's warehouse for inventory," she said. I sipped the coffee and grabbed my cell phone to call Amadi.

"I don't know if I can make it. I feel like shit," I said and she laughed.

"You really got it bad for Kanye. You were moaning his name in your sleep. You didn't tell me all of the details about the night you two went to the party. What happened afterwards?" she asked.

"After the party, we went home. I don't remember really because I think I got drunk. I need to stay away from alcohol. I've been sneaking and drinking since age ten and I think it's ruining my memory. I feel like I'm missing something," I said and she smiled.

"You are just enjoying the life, that's all," she said. After I finished my coffee, I took a shower and grabbed the change of clothes I kept at her apartment. I left out of the building and headed straight to my car.

"I definitely need to stop drinking. I don't remember driving last night," I said aloud and started my car then headed home.

Osiris

I paced back and forth inside the sanctuary I spent my nights in. Meda sat on the red couch and laughed at me. The sounds of her laugh caused my ears to bleed.

"Stop it! You are a rotten bitch! You've been planning this for a long time. You disguised yourself? I cannot believe you!" I yelled at her.

"All you need is more blood so the dark side of you will surface. Stop being a wimp and get over it," she spat.

"Every time I drink blood I turn into something evil. When I don't drink it, I can feel my feelings again," I said. A force slammed me into the wall and a thick vine appeared from the cracks inside the floor. It slithered up my body and wrapped around my neck.

"If you don't drink, the deal is off! I will kill you and your parents and rule Anubi myself after Goon is dead. You will drink every time you get thirsty for it," she said and the vine disappeared.

"They are innocent, Meda. I am innocent, and you gave me this evil spirit and it's feeding on me like I'm dead! I want my life back!" I yelled and she smirked.

"You will have it all back after you finish the task I gave to you. I know what will make you feel better," she said and left the room. When she came back, she had a young woman with her. Meda pushed her onto the floor and the girl cried.

"Please take me back home. My baby needs me," she pleaded with tears falling from her eyes. Meda gripped the girl's hair and yanked her head back, exposing her neck. The girl tried to get away from Meda, but she pulled her hair tighter.

"Look at that beautiful vein going down her neck. It's time to feed, so do it!" she shouted.

"NO!" I yelled. Meda pulled out a gold dagger and ran it across the girl's neck. Her blood dripped onto her pale yellow top and my teeth came through my gums. My nails sharpened and my stomach tightened.

"Drink it!" she said. The smell of fresh blood pulled me in and before I knew it, I was sucking on the dying girl's neck. I sucked every drop until her lifeless eyes stared up at the ceiling. I stood up and I felt that high again. I tossed her body out of the window of the abandoned building. After Meda disappeared, I took a shower and headed out to the club. I went to the clubs to scope out my next target. It was usually a woman who aroused me. I seduced her with my charm and she would invite me to her house. Once she gave her body to me, I sucked the soul out of her.

I walked through the crowd and the sounds of beating hearts filled my ears more than the club's music. I wore black fitted jeans, a black V-neck shirt and a black leather jacket. I wore a pair of black Jordan's on my feet that the humans went crazy over. It didn't take long to figure out the fashion. I ordered a drink.

"Patrón with ice and extra salt on the rim," I said to the bartender. When I looked to my right, an ebony beauty was standing next to me, wearing a short, red dress. The dress showed a lot of cleavage.

"You look beautiful tonight, my queen," I said to her and she blushed.

"Thank you, you look nice yourself. I love that necklace," she said eyeing my jewelry. I traced my finger around her neck.

"It would look even better on you. What are you drinking tonight?" I asked.

"Champagne," she said. I ordered a bottle of champagne and she was smitten by me already.

I might not need to use my charm after all, I thought. My erection swelled inside of my pants and I wanted to take her right there but I couldn't.

I saw a familiar face walking toward the bar; I knew him from school.

"Aye, man, aren't you the new kid on campus? You moved here from Africa, right?" he asked me.

"Yes, and you are?" I asked.

"Yardi and you are Osiris? Damn, man, that jewelry is fire," he said. I could tell that he was slightly buzzed from his drink.

I would like to get a chain like that. If only I had the money. I used the money I had saved to buy that bitch Monifa a necklace she hasn't worn yet. What an ungrateful bitch! Yardi ranted inside his head.

"Meet in the bathroom by the library at school tomorrow at one o'clock and I will give you the hook up," I said and he beamed with excitement.

Greedy human, I thought.

"Good looking out," he said and patted my shoulder. I grabbed the ebony beauty by the hand and led her to a quieter spot of the club.

"You sell jewelry?" she asked me.

"No, but I will if someone needs it. But tell me a little about yourself, beautiful," I said. My eyes gazed over her curves and she blushed.

"No one has ever looked at me that way before," she said and pressed her body closer to mine.

"Who are you here with?" I asked.

"My friend but she went outside to talk to her boyfriend. She might not come back. They are known for screwing everywhere," she said and laughed.

"What are you known for besides being extremely sexy?" I replied. Her hand went to my erection and she squeezed it.

"Making your wildest dreams come true if the price is right," she said.

"Price is right?" I asked.

"You have to pay to play, baby," she said.

I will play, but by the time I'm done with you, I won't be paying for anything, I thought. An hour later after the champagne was gone, we left the club. I waved down a taxi and when he stopped, I opened the door for the woman. I didn't ask her name and I didn't care to ask because she was going to be dead by the end of the night.

My hand slid up her thick thigh and up her dress.

"Naughty boy," she laughed. I fondled her in the backseat and she moaned. I caressed her breast.

"It feels so good, babyyy," she moaned when I sucked her neck. I slid my finger inside of her and she wasn't as tight as the female wolves I bedded in Anubi.

"I live right here," I said and the cab driver stopped. I placed a few bills in his hand.

"Thanks for the lovely tip, sir. You and the lovely lady have a good night," the old white man said. I helped the woman in the red dress out of the cab and she looked around.

"This place is deserted. I thought you lived downtown in the new lofts where the rich people live," she said.

"You will be surprised," I said and grabbed her hand. We walked into the old building with vines growing out of the windows.

"This place stinks," she said and covered her nose.

I need to get rid of those bodies underneath the floor, I thought. We stepped onto the elevator and I pulled the door down. She looked terrified but it didn't matter. I only wanted pleasure and her blood. When the elevator opened, we stepped off and she covered her mouth.

"Wow, this is beautiful. It looks like something from the dark times," she said when she looked around. I had candles around the room with a bed in the middle. The bed had red sheets with gold curtains draped over the bed post. The dead roses crunched underneath her heels as she looked around.

"Get naked," I said.

"Are you going to give me a tour?" she asked.

"That's not what we agreed on. I pay to play, so get naked," I said. She kicked her heels off and I picked her up.

"You're strong," she said. I tossed her on the bed and ripped her dress off. I took my shirt off and she spread her legs. She rubbed her pink bud waiting for me to enter her while I took the rest of my clothes off. Once I was naked, I pulled her to the end of my bed. I pushed her legs up.

"We need a condom," she said.

"What is that?" I asked.

"For protection," she said.

"Immortals don't carry diseases or get them," I replied. I traced the head of my shaft up and down her slit before I entered her. I slid all the way into her and she screamed.

"It's too big, slow down!" she said and pushed me back.

Take all of me, and besides, you are not that tight! I said in her thoughts. She laid still and let me have my way with her. She was hypnotized. Chancy's face appeared in my head and my erection grew harder. I pumped in and out of the stranger and her eyes rolled into the back of her head. I picked her up and slid her up and down my full length and she was dripping. She had two orgasms since I entered her. I grabbed her by the neck and my nails sharpened. Blood trickled down her breast and I tasted it. She must have been caught up in the pleasure I was giving her because she didn't feel it. Small lines of blood seeped down her chest and I exploded. Her nipples hardened as I throbbed inside of her. My teeth expanded and it pierced through her neck. She gasped for air as I slowly sucked her soul out of her body. After I was finished, I dropped her onto the floor. I sat in the chair in the corner of my room and thought about Chancy. I wanted to feel her. The evil that lurked inside of me wanted to taste her blood but I didn't want to. I just wanted to be with her and hear her laughs, admire her smile, and feel the warmth of her body against my cold body.

****

The next day...

"Are you sure about this?" Yardi asked while I held the tubes Meda wanted me to steal from a lab in my hand.

"Sell it for forty bucks, it's legit," I said.

"This shit is worth thousands I heard," he replied.

"I know but what's the purpose of stealing them if you are going to sell them at whole price?" I asked. I pulled out a needle and he jumped.

"What are you doing?" he asked.

"I took the serum and now it's your turn," I said.

"Nigga, I'm not taking this shit. Does it even work?" he asked. My eyes turned red and my teeth sharpened. I dug my nails into his neck and blood trickled down my hand from the wound.

"Take the fucking serum or you will become my meal. Which one do you want?" I asked and dropped him on the floor. I tossed the needle at him. His hands shook when he held up the tube. He dipped the needle into the top of the tube and the serum filled the needle. He rolled up his sleeve and stuck the needle into his vein. A few seconds later, his arm bubbled and his body fell over. He jerked and blood filled his eyes. His back raised up off the floor and it snapped. His neck snapped and his teeth pierced through his gums. His body turned gray and his ears pulled the skin on his face back. He gasped before he went limp and his body went back to normal. I could no longer hear his heart beat because he had turned into a vampire and beast hybrid from the serum that had my blood mixed inside of it.

Excellent, Meda said.

Get the hell out of my head! I yelled. I opened the window and tossed Yardi out after I made sure the coast was clear. I jumped out behind him. I threw him over my shoulder and went to the big flower bush behind the building. I laid him in the bush because I didn't want someone to come into the bathroom and see him dead. I covered him up with my jacket and went to my next class.

****

"Hey, Osiris. Wait up!" a voice called from behind me. It was Chancy. I hadn't been seeing much of her because I skipped the class I had with her.

"Hey, beautiful. I don't think your boyfriend wants me around you," I said and she giggled.

"I can have friends, plus I enjoyed your company. Do you want to grab a bite to eat?" she asked.

"I'm not hungry but I can watch you eat," I replied. I followed her to her car and got in when she unlocked the door. When she got inside, she just stared at me.

"There is something different about you. You talk different and you are acting normal. What happened?" she asked and started the car up.

"I picked up on a lot of things," I answered.

I hope Yardi stays there until I get back, I thought.

"Why did you lie about where you came from?" she asked.

"I didn't want to scare anybody. I'm aware of the truce between my father and his brother, Goon. Anubi beasts stay in Anubi and Goon's pack stays here," I answered.

"I'm glad you came," she said. Shame filled my heart when I thought about all of the chaos I was causing by turning humans into vampire and beast hybrids. I didn't have a choice because my soul belonged to a demon. The car came to a red light and I caressed her face. She wanted to pull back but she was attracted to me as much as I was attracted to her.

"I wish there was a world for me and you with just us two in it. No traditions, no lies, no guilt, nothing. We would be able to explore each other's bodies under the moon. That's a vision I have of me and you," I said. She pulled away and looked down.

"Our worlds are different. Eventually, you will have to go back to your kingdom," she said. The sound of her heart beating thumped in my ears. I felt my fangs expand and that evil part of me was trying to take over. It wanted to suck her blood until she took her last breath. It wanted to make love to her while killing her. Her death would've been a pleasurable one. My fangs went away after I fought the urge to bite her.

"I want to see your beast," she said.

"My beast was taken away from me temporarily. I wasn't obedient with Anubi's strict laws. My mother is a witch and she put a spell on me," I said and she laughed.

"I can't picture you misbehaving. How does it feel not having it?" she asked.

"I felt empty until I met you, of course."

"I see the charm is in full effect. I cannot imagine not being a beast," she said.

"Your beast is beautiful. I saw you in the woods, hunting. Your beast is very aggressive and it reminded me of the warriors back home," I said.

"You saw me naked?" she asked.

"Yes, but I was more interested in your beast," I replied and she blushed. She pulled up to a small restaurant.

"What is Goon like?" I asked.

"Stubborn, mean, over-protective, and impatient but his heart is filled with love. He took in my mother and oldest sister into the pack after they ran from their pack for being mistreated. I will do anything for him because if he didn't take my mother in, she wouldn't have met my father," she said. We got out of the car and headed inside the restaurant. We talked for an hour and a half before she took me back to campus. We sat in her car in the parking lot.

"No more secrets," Chancy said.

"No more secrets," I lied. I pulled her face to mine and kissed her lips. She tensed up until I grabbed the back of her head and slipped my tongue into her mouth. Her heart was beating fast and I could hear the blood flowing through her veins—it was calling me. My hand slid down to her breast and she growled. My erection pressed against my jeans and I wanted so badly to enter her.

"We need to stop," she said. I slid my hand up her skirt and she was bare. My middle finger entered her warm, wet tightness and she moaned. Seconds later, the windows shattered in the car and my body was yanked out by a force. I flew into a tree in the woods by the parking lot. Akea appeared in front of me and he slammed me into a tree.

"Stay away from her!" he said to me. I punched him in the face and he slid back. Three electric bolts struck my body and I grimaced in pain. I charged into him and he disappeared. A force slammed me from behind, face down. Akea grabbed the back of my neck and tossed me into the air then another bolt struck me.

"STOP IT!" Chancy screamed.

"I told you to stay away from that blood sucka. He is up to no good," he said while Chancy helped me up. I was very weak and blood was going to be the cure.

"You don't know what you are talking about! You have visions but that doesn't mean they are true," she yelled at him.

"My visions let me see what is to come in the future and he is going to turn you into one of those if you become intimate with him. He is a vampire and his charm is what is reeling you in. He is going to wait until you fall for him just so that he can kill you," Akea said and I laughed.

"Son of a bitch! You don't know what you are talking about," I spat.

"You sound like a human on Earth. I guess that comes from drinking all of the human blood. You are what you eat," he said. I wished it was that simple because I had beast blood in Anubi before I came to Earth and it didn't do anything. Chancy pulled away from me and I grabbed her arm.

"Don't believe him. He is jealous of us," I said and Akea laughed. Chancy had feelings for the both of us but maybe Akea was right, my charm was reeling her in.

"What are you and don't lie to me?" she said and I didn't answer.

"I am an immortal and that's all you need to know. I don't have to explain myself to you or anyone else. I have not harmed you. You figure out what you think I am," I said. I looked at Akea and his blue eyes glowed.

"I guess your beast was taken away from you, too, witch! Your fancy little spells and fancy lightning. I almost thought you were my mother," I teased and he laughed.

I walked away from them and out of the woods. I sat on top of the school building for a few hours. The moon peaked over the clouds and it was time. I jumped off the building and headed to the bush where I hid Yardi's body. He was slightly moving and I dragged him out of the bush. I lifted up his eyelids and his eyes had a spec of red. I slapped his face.

"Wake up, it's time to hunt," I said. He sat up and looked around.

"I had the craziest dream," he said and slowly got up.

"Tell me about it later, we need to get out of here," I said. I heard whistling and a heartbeat. The beating thumped in my ears. Yardi's red eyes glowed; he was ready for his first taste of blood. The whistling got louder and I heard something being dragged across the ground. A janitor came around the corner pulling a mop bucket behind him.

"School hours are over. What are you two doing out here this time of night on campus? There isn't any funny business going on, is it?" he asked.

Suck his blood and do it now. Drink until his heart stops, I said. Yardi's teeth sharpened before he charged into the janitor. The janitor screamed when Yardi's teeth pierced his neck. The smell of fresh blood leaking onto the grass filled my nostrils. Yardi drank until the man stopped moving.

Get rid of the body. He picked up the dead man's body and threw him over his shoulder. He walked to the dumpster behind the building and dropped him inside of it. I didn't want to harm anyone from Goon's pack even though I was forced to, but I had hatred in my heart for Akea. Whether he liked it or not, Chancy was mine and I wanted him dead.

The Underworld has your soul now. There is no more fighting with it. Once hate fills your heart, the demon inside of you, rules you, Meda said.

Shut up, bitch! I spat.

Akea

"I keep telling you he is bad for you," I said to Chancy after we got home. She was lying across her bed with her eyes closed. She was ignoring me but I was concerned about her, especially because of the dream I had. It was a message and I believed in all of my visions. I believed that somewhere in me existed a beast and I believed that Osiris was sent to Earth to destroy our pack.

"Get out of my room, Akea," she said. Since the night at the club, me and Chancy started dating and doing things together. I was pissed off that she let Osiris touch her but it wasn't her fault, and her liking him was all an illusion. Vampires were seductive and deceiving.

"Don't say I didn't warn you," I said and walked out of the room. When I got to my bedroom, my brother was sitting at my desk, going through my spell books. I closed them shut and he chuckled.

"Ease up, bro, I was just curious," he said.

"What do you want?" I asked.

"Loosen up, I got something for you," he said and handed me a blunt. He lit it for me and I puffed on it.

"Remember the wolf men I was telling you about?" he asked.

"Yeah, what about them?" I replied.

"I'm telling you this isn't just a coincidence. The beast is going to be used for something like puppets. I feel it in my spirit," he said. Kanye didn't have visions the way I did. He felt it instead of seeing it.

"People have been using science for years to create things. This time it's for human pleasure. It's sick but, bro, a lot of women crave animalistic sex and it sells. Okay, so one of them got out of hand in your building, but that doesn't have anything to do with us. Arya said a lot of women are enjoying it, so let it go," I said. He banged on my desk and it split in half.

"Muthafucka, get your magical ass out of the clouds. Those beasts are the enemy. My beast knows it and I know it. Every time I see one, I have to kill it. We need to find the source," he said and pulled out a flyer from his back pocket.

"What is this?" I asked.

"It's the same flyer Arya had when she and I went to that show. We need to be at the show tonight and get down to the root of this," he said.

"I don't want to see a lab-created beast fuck a human, bro," I said and he grabbed me by the shirt. He yanked me out of the chair and slammed me against the wall.

"I just gave your weird ass the last bit of my good kush. You are coming with me," he spat. I pushed him away and fixed my shirt.

"Alright, I will go, but I'm warning you. If I see something I don't like, I'm disappearing," I said.

"Be ready tonight. I got an outfit for you downstairs," he said and left my room.

****

A few hours later, I was showered and dressed. I wore a pair of denim jeans, a fitted casual top, and a pair of Timbs. Kanye nodded his head with approval. He handed me a big face gold watch that was covered in diamonds.

"This watch didn't hit the stores yet, so thank me later," he said after I put it around my wrist. Chancy came into the living room wearing ripped tight jeans and a half turtle-neck top, showing off her curves. Her hair was braided into an up-do and she wore a little jewelry.

"I don't like him looking like you. He looks like a drug dealer," Chancy fussed to Kanye.

"A nigga tried to buy you with jewels. How do you feel about that? Because if I was you, I wouldn't be saying shit. Akea will stick out like sore thumb walking into that show looking like a private detective. They might think he is an undercover cop," he said and she growled at him.

"Stop being such a dick!" she yelled at him.

"I will when you appreciate what you have instead of that weird-ass nigga you keep getting caught with," Kanye spat.

"Bro, chill," I said and his eyes turned blue.

"Okay, I will for now," he said and Chancy balled up her fists.

"What do you know about appreciating someone?" Chancy asked.

"That's between me and my mate," Kanye replied. Zaan, Baneet, and Monifa came down the stairs. Monifa went over to Kanye and kissed his cheek. His hands roamed over her bottom and she started blushing.

"This is weird seeing the two of you all lovey dovey," Baneet said.

"We still hate each other sometimes," Monifa replied.

"Yeah, she still acts stuck up but all I have to do is touch her spot and she get all w—" Monifa covered his mouth.

"Damn it, Kanye, stop telling our business!" she yelled at him.

"Ugh, thank God Zaan is passionate and respects our love life," Baneet bragged.

"Hell, I will be scared to disrespect you, too, if you were treating me like a dog from the kennel wearing muzzles and shit," Kanye said and Monifa elbowed him. Kanye was an asshole and if he and I weren't twins, he could've passed for being Izra's pup.

"Ugh, Monifa did you tell Kanye our secret? It was between us," Baneet said to Monifa.

"No, she didn't tell me. I saw when y'all was talking about it the other day," Kanye said.

"I hope you get eaten by a grizzly bear," Baneet replied and stormed out of the house with Zaan following behind her. Chancy grabbed my hand and pulled me out of the house.

"I'm riding with you," Chancy said.

****

The party was an hour away from our mansion.

"This place is spooky," Chancy said. Kanye was in front of me in his sports car and Baneet's truck followed behind me. We were going down a long, dark road in the woods.

"Tell me about it," I said. We drove further into the woods until we came to an old mansion with cracked lion statues in front of it. A lot of cars were parked along the road and I could hear the music coming from inside. We exited our vehicles.

"This shit is crazy," Zaan said, looking around. Baneet pulled Zaan closer to her.

"I know you are not scared, Baneet. We are wolves, honey. Nothing puts fear in our beasts," Chancy said.

"Shut up, Chancy. I'm not scared," Baneet said and I laughed.

"Let's go," Kanye said and pushed the black gate open. We walked up the old steps to the front door. Two large men, wearing all-black with shades on, guarded the door. They patted us down before the door opened for us to go in. When I walked in, it was rowdy. A few Caucasian girls sat on swings that hung from the ceiling and they were naked.

"Is that Sarah Baxter?" Chancy asked.

"No, that's not her. Why do you keep bringing her up? I'm dating you unless you know something that I don't know," I said.

"That is Sarah, look a little closer," she said. Sarah swung over my head, and when she came back, our eyes connected. She tried to cover herself up but it was too late. I was somewhat pissed off that she was showing everything that she shared with me at one point.

"I keep bringing her up because you still have feelings for her," Chancy said before she walked away. Monifa and Baneet followed behind her.

"What's up with Chancy?" Zaan asked.

"She thinks I'm still into Sarah," I replied.

"Well, are you? Because your eyes are glowing and you look pissed off," Kanye replied.

"You two wouldn't understand," I said. Sarah got off the swing and grabbed a silk robe from a table. She walked through the crowd headed toward me.

"Pimp slap her ass as soon as she gets close enough to reach," Kanye joked and Zaan laughed—they were high.

"Can I talk to you for a second?" Sarah asked.

Bro, Chancy is staring at you and her eyes are glowing. If you don't want Sarah to look like shredded mozzarella cheese, I suggest you stay put and talk to her here, Kanye said.

"What's up?" I asked.

"Can we talk in private?" she replied.

Don't do it! Zaan said and Kanye shook his head.

It's innocent, I replied and walked off. We stood in a hallway and it was just us two.

"I wasn't expecting you to come to a party like this," she said.

"What are you doing here?" I asked and she looked away. A tear fell from her eye and she wiped it away.

"I need the extra money. I'm going to get paid for doing a show. It's a part of an experiment. It's totally harmless," she said.

"Do you know what they are?" I asked.

"Yes, this is my second show. I have to pay for college. I'm not rich like you. It's just a fantasy and it doesn't last long," she said.

"You could've come to me. I would've given you the money," I replied.

"I was too embarrassed," she said and wrapped her arms around me.

"I love you, Akea, and seeing you with Chancy is killing me. Can we fix us? I know you still have feelings for me," she cried. Seconds later, she pulled away from me and kissed me. Her robe flew open and her small but round breasts pressed against my chest. The strawberry shampoo she used tickled my nose. I heard heels clicking down the hall and when I looked up, Chancy was strutting towards us with glowing eyes.

"It's not what you think," I said.

"Great, so you wouldn't mind if I had her for supper?" she seethed.

Stop before you shift in front of her, I said.

So what, she likes to get fucked by beasts anyway. That's why she's here, right? Too bad you don't have what it takes to be a beast, Chancy replied.

And a blood sucka does? I spat and she pushed me. Sarah took off running down the hall.

"Stop acting ghetto!" I yelled.

"You would say that after fucking someone like Sarah. You can't handle me," Chancy said and stormed off.

"I didn't mean it like that!" I called after her.

"Fuck you!" she yelled back. Dealing with Chancy was getting complicated. I liked her a lot and even though I still felt something for Sarah, I wasn't going back to her in that way. Chancy was a challenge and she brought out another side of me.

I found Zaan and Kanye by the drink table. I fixed myself a drink thought I didn't know what I was drinking, but I needed something to keep me from bursting.

"Calm down, bro," Kanye said as I guzzled the clear liquid. It burned my chest and throat.

"Chancy is driving me insane. She just gets me so mad where I feel like exploding and wrapping my hands around her neck. Why do females have to be so complicated?" I asked.

"She ain't complicated, she just ain't what you are used to. Get a little rough with her. Jack her up and show her whose dick is swinging—you are the warrior. Bite her one good time," Kanye replied.

"I'm not a beast," I said.

"You ain't got to be a beast to bite a muthafucka. Humans bite each other all of the time during sex. It might not be our type of bite, but you got teeth, use them," he said.

"Don't listen to this fool," Zaan said.

"What are you guys doing here?" a voice said from behind us. When I turned around, it was Arya and her friend Laura that we only saw a few times.

"What are you doing here?" Kanye asked.

"I came with Laura. I wanted to see what all the talk was about," she replied.

"You know what it's about. We just went to a show like this a week ago," Kanye said.

"What show?" she asked.

"The show with the wolf men. The one you said that was for fantasy purposes. We talked about it in the kitchen the morning after you and Kanye went out," I said.

"Are you guys drunk? What the hell are you two talking about? Kanye and I went to a party and came home," she said.

"Ummm, excuse me, but Arya's been partying a lot lately. It was nice seeing you all, but we need to get good seats," Laura said and pulled Arya away from us and through the crowd.

"Something is up with that. Arya doesn't know what the hell we were just talking about. She knows darn-well that we went to the same show and we even fooled around," Kanye fussed.

"Something is up with that," I replied. A few seconds later, a man came onto the stage and announced that the show was ready to start. Sarah and a few other females walked out onto the stage and it reminded me of an auction. She was selling her body to a generic beast. I lost focus of everything around me when five men with gray, stringy hair covering their bodies and wolf faces walked across the stage. The audience grew quiet.

It's so quiet you can hear a roach pissing, Kanye thought.

"I would like to introduce everyone to the LOBO brand where fantasy takes you to another world. A world filled with sexual men with beastly desires," the spokesman said and the crowd clapped.

"I'm going to puke if I stand here and watch this. Bro, this is bestiality," I said.

"Sarah Baxter is up there looking like *Little Red Riding Hood*. After that thing stretches her vagina out, you might need to use some magic to get it tight again. There is no way her small pussy can take that beast," Kanye said.

"It is a small pussy. Wolf pussy sits open like the fattest peach known to man. It's pretty and juicy like a grapefruit," Zaan said.

The women on the stage and the beast started to go at it. Two wolf men grabbed Sarah and she seemed to enjoy their long, drooling tongues and slimy-like faces. The wolf men had Sarah sandwiched, one entered her from the back and the other entered her from the front. Their big hands groped at her and squeezed her breasts. Screams filled the house from the intense pleasure the beast was giving the women on stage.

"Is it just me or does it look like two slices of molded bread with a piece of Swiss cheese in the middle?" Kanye asked referring to Sarah being in the middle of the two beasts. Zaan howled in laughter. The screams got higher and I saw Sarah dripping with blood. The doors burst open and when I turned around, there were six wolf men with red eyes and very sharp teeth standing at the entrance.

"ARRGHHHHHHHHHHHHH!" a woman screamed. She was being mauled to death on stage.

"These muthafuckas are something else!" Kanye said and his eyes started changing. The people in the audience started screaming and running out of the house. A few more beasts appeared out of nowhere and started attacking the humans, like they were meals. Kanye and Zaan shifted and I heard howls coming from the other end of the house. Chancy, Monifa, and Baneet were already in beast form. I turned the beast that was killing Sarah into ashes. I floated in the air to avoid getting trampled over. A few wolves from different packs shifted but they weren't a match for the wolf men. The wolf men shredded one werewolf in half. I sent the wolf man flying across the room and he slammed into the wall, shattering like glass. Kanye and Zaan were pulling both ends of a wolf man and he split in two. I had never seen so much blood in all of my life. Blood was everywhere and the smell filled the air. A few humans in the crowd turned to wolf men and I realized it was a set up. The whole party was used to attack humans like they were meals and we put a dent into their plans—they were angry at us. Arya was out in the crowd helping Baneet fight off a wolf man. Monifa was dragging one of them up the wall by its neck and slung him out of the window. I tried to get to Sarah but I had to help my pack. When I finally got to the stage, Sarah was gone. Half of the wolf men were dead and the other half ran off into the night. On our way leaving out of the old mansion, I spotted the spokesman lying in the middle of the floor, bleeding to death. He was trying to talk.

"My name is Jose and I worked for the brand. There is something wrong with it. Take this list; it has every male name on it that was part of the experiment," he said and coughed up blood.

"Who did you work for?" I asked.

"La—" he said then he started choking on his blood and seconds later, he died.

****

An hour later...

"Those are some ugly, rabies-looking, funny-shaped muthafuckas. It looked like someone photo shopped their heads," Kanye vented.

"They were past ugly, them things were hideous," I replied.

"We should move out, too, Zaan," Baneet said. We were all at Kanye's and Monifa's place.

"Would I still have to wear a muzzle if we do?" Zaan asked with sarcasm in his voice.

"Were you really cool with that?" Kanye asked Zaan.

"Mind your business, Kanye. This has nothing to do with you. Your only concern is Monifa," Baneet spat.

"It doesn't have nothing to do with me because if it did, you wouldn't be sitting here. That's a disgrace to our tradition. Dayo will have to get over it after Zaan marks you," Kanye replied.

"Dayo and Izra are two different wolves. My father will kill me and Zaan," Baneet said.

"I keep telling her that she needs to stop," Chancy said.

"I know you didn't just speak on this matter. You were feeling Akea and after he gave you the attention you wanted, you went to the blood sucka. You and your sisters got some issues," Kanye fussed then took a swig from his Hennessy bottle—he was drunk.

"Babe, stop," Monifa said.

"He thinks he is the love doctor because he is developing his disgusting wolf serum to mate with. Just a few weeks ago, you didn't like Monifa, but now all of sudden you want to be like Romeo and Juliet," Chancy said.

"My wolf serum is far from disgusting, blood sucka. Who said I hated Monifa?" Kanye replied. He never hated Monifa. He had a crush on Arya but it went away because he fell in love with Monifa and that was eight years ago.

"Kanye is just a fucking jerk," Baneet said and he growled at her.

"Can you all just shut up!" Monifa said.

"I will not shut up because Kanye always gets the chance to speak his mind. Why can't we ever have a voice?" Baneet asked.

"Y'all are buzzing my high," Zaan said.

"You need to take up for me!" Baneet yelled at Zaan.

"It's hard to when I'm not connected to you. All we do is sneak around and fuck like some teenage humans. It's getting boring," Zaan fussed. Baneet jumped on him from across the table and knocked him down onto the floor. She scratched his face and bit him. He grabbed her by the neck and sent her sailing across the room. Chancy growled at Zaan and she tried to charge into him. I put a shield in front of him and she slid back into the wall with rope tied around her.

"Let me go, Akea! And get this rope off of me!" she yelled and I ignored her. I was still pissed off about her and Osiris and the argument we had at the party. Zaan walked over to Baneet and picked her up.

"I didn't mean it," he said and she snatched away from him.

"We are over!" she yelled before she stormed out of house.

"Appreciate the hospitality, but I'm going to leave. I gotta make sure she gets home safe," Zaan said and rushed out behind her. I let Chancy loose and she fell onto the floor. She wanted to attack me.

"Don't you even think about it," I spat. Kanye and Monifa were in the kitchen and Monifa was giggling.

I need some pussy. Do you think I should kick them out or do you want to sneak off? I caught an earful of their conversation.

"Bro, really? We can still hear your thoughts. I'm out," I said.

Chancy said goodbye to Monifa and gave Kanye the middle finger on our way out the door. I walked down the flight of steps and her heels clicked behind me.

"I guess you are going to stay mad at me," she said.

"I'm not thinking about that," I replied. She grabbed my hand and turned me around.

"I'm sorry, Akea," she said.

"I distanced myself from you when I noticed you was liking me because I was afraid I couldn't give you what you wanted. I can't bite you and make you feel passion. It held me back from you, but seeing you and Osiris together opened my eyes. It's not your fault, it's mine. Too bad Osiris's intentions are not the right ones," I replied. We stood on the sidewalk without saying anything. I stared into her eyes and it was like looking into windows of her life. I regretted shutting the pack out because I didn't feel complete with myself. From that moment on, I accepted who I was and what I was a part of.

"What are you staring at?" Chancy asked me.

"I'm staring at my future," I said and her smile lit up like the streetlights.

"Are you trying to charm me out of my panties, Akea?" she asked.

"You don't wear panties often," I replied and she slapped my arm and I almost tipped over.

"How would you know?" she asked.

"I know a lot of things. I can see through your eyes what you like," I replied.

"You are such a nerd," she teased. We started walking and she put her arm through mine. I looked down into her delicate face and I forgot about Sarah being missing and the wolf men.

When we finally got home, it was late. I was glad that the rest of the pack was asleep. I went down to my hall and Chancy went down to hers. I turned around and she was standing in front of her bedroom door.

Good night, she said.

Good night.

****

After I showered, I collapsed onto my bed, naked. The weed, the fight, and the small amount of alcohol I had took over my body. I dozed off for a few hours and was awakened when a figure crawled onto my bed. I sat up and Chancy's beast's eyes glowed at me. She wore a long, white silk robe and I could see that she was naked underneath.

"What are you doing? It's late," I said and she pushed me down onto the bed. She straddled me and opened up her robe. A tribal marking traveled down her cleavage and stopped above her pussy. She was dripping on my leg from between her slit.

"I couldn't sleep, Akea," she said and dug her nails into my chest. My dick pressed against her center.

"I don't think, ahhhhhhhhh—" I moaned out. She slowly slid down my girth. I sat up and wrapped my arms around her body and pulled her grape-sized nipple into my mouth. Her growls mixed with moans filled the room. I took us to paradise. We were on a beach just us two. The waves came up on the sand and washed over my body. I sucked harder on her nipple and her pussy squeezed my dick.

"OHHHHH, you are so big!" she moaned and thrust her hips forward. We were still in my bedroom, but our minds were someplace else. It felt so real that I could smell the milk from the coconuts on the island. I leaned back and slowly moved her hips forward while I thrust upwards into her. Her essence dripped down my dick and her moans grew louder.

"AHHHHHHHHHHH," I groaned when I bounced her up and down. She was screaming my name and her long, sharp nails scratched my chest.

"You are about to make me cum! Fuck me harder!" she moaned. I rolled her over and bent her knees. I held her bent knees down and opened her legs until her pussy lips spread apart from each other. I slowly entered her and watched her small hole open up for me and I wanted to release. Sweat dripped down her chest and her body grew hot. I raised up and pounded her into the sand. Her essence spilled over—she was over flowing. She bit my shoulder, piercing through my skin and her nails dug into my back and drew blood. I pounded into her harder. My testicles slapped against her flesh. I whispered to her.

"I can't bite you but I want you to feel me," I said. She screamed out but I kissed her. I was using my magic to make her take more of me. I entered a place through her pussy that had never been reached, a place that a human couldn't experience. I made myself grow inside of her, I was in her womb. She howled when I continued to pump into her but only I could hear her howls. I didn't want her to wake up anyone in the house. Her body trembled underneath my touch and she squirted. I groaned into her ear when I jerked and released inside of her. I would've killed Sarah if I would've used my magic on her. I didn't naturally grow during sex but I had the ability to do everything to Chancy to please her. To make her forget about Osiris and make her stay away from him. After I was finished, I collapsed on top of her sweaty chest. She rubbed my back and I drifted off into a deep sleep.

****

The next day...

When I woke up, Chancy wasn't in my bed, but she left me a note:

Good morning sleepy head. I had to go to dance practice. It's over at 1pm, so be there outside waiting for me or else...

P.S
We are a couple now so don't screw with my emotions!

I chuckled and put the note inside my nightstand. I shower and got dressed. I was headed to Kanye's home.

****

"I have all of the names of the people who were experimented on. I noticed that nobody on the list was over the age of thirty. It seems to me that the serum works better on young males," I said to Kanye. He was sitting on the couch inside of his condo, playing a video game with a blunt hanging out of his mouth.

"We need to figure out how to reverse it," he replied.

"That's just it. I don't think it can be reversed. Once the serum is inside of their body, it spreads immediately. It has the ability to make the human stronger, look younger and healthier. It's hard to reverse something that is used for multiple reasons. The serum can do a lot for humans," I replied and he dropped his controller.

"We have to kill everyone on that list," he said.

"I wanted to figure out another way but death is our only option. If this shit spreads, it can wipe us out. If they reproduce, it will become worse. The food supply for the werewolves will decrease. I'm with you on this one because they need to be stopped," I replied. Monifa came out of the bedroom wearing a robe.

"I'm helping out," she said and Kanye growled.

"This is a man's job, beautiful," he replied and she mushed him on the back of his head.

"I didn't ask you, I was telling you; so, therefore, your two cents are not needed. When are we making our move, Akea?" she asked me.

"Nigga, you better not answer her and block your thoughts so she won't figure it out," Kanye said.

"Traitor," she said to him and walked away.

"I can be that because your ass ain't going!" he called out after her.

"You sounded like Father," I said.

"I'm going to turn into Father if she keeps testing my beast. But what's up with you? I noticed your walk when you came in. You know the walk after getting some good pussy," he said.

"I had an entertaining night," I said.

"You found Sarah Baxter? You ain't never wore a pair of sweatpants before," he said.

"It was with Chancy," I said and he coughed on his weed smoke. He passed the blunt to me.

"I noticed something last night. The wolf men were different from the one upstairs and the one at the show Arya took me to. The wolf men last night were stronger and they had red eyes like Osiris. They weren't eating the humans; they were drinking their blood like a vampire bat. I think he has something to do with this. Matter of fact, I can feel that he does. He is the only immortal with red eyes," Kanye said.

The doorbell rang and Kanye got up to answer it. Seconds later, our father walked into the living room wearing an all-black suit with a thick gold necklace around his neck. The necklace had a pyramid medallion on it. I dropped my blunt on the floor and his ice blue eyes glowed when he growled at me. He picked the blunt up and it disappeared in his hand.

"Come on, Pops. We weren't done with that," Kanye said.

"Glad to see you two getting along," he said and looked around Kanye's and Monifa's home.

"Nice but this is only temporarily. Pack rules are pack rules, and we don't leave each other. The only reason I agreed with your mother to let you come here is because we don't want to hear the two of you mating in the house," he said.

"Me and Monifa are not pups anymore," Kanye said.

"It doesn't matter what age you are. We are a pack and we stay together. It's been in our tradition for thousands of years. The reason for this visit is because my two sons are hiding something from me," he said and sat down across from me. Monifa dropped her pitcher of water and disappeared out of the kitchen.

I'm her soulmate and she just leaves my black ass out to dry, Kanye thought and I chuckled. I was feeling the effects from the blunt we smoked.

"Nothing is going on," Kanye said.

"Lie to me again, Kanye. I saw your visions this morning. There's a new breed of beast and you knew about it for some time. Tell me why me and the rest of my pack brothers don't know about it? Are you taking the lead without telling me?" our father asked.

"No, but since I'm next up to be alpha, I figured I'll deal with it myself. There's a lot going on and I didn't want you to go back to Anubi. Mother said if you go back, it will be hard to come back home. The portal doesn't open for years and sometimes magic can't even open it," he answered.

"My nephew, Osiris, is on Earth. I it saw through your vision. Where is his aunt, Meda?" he asked.

"Meda?" I asked.

"This is too much shit to discuss right now. It happened twenty years ago. I killed my father because he made a deal with an ancient warlock name, Musaf. Musaf wanted to be born again because he was too old and his spells were getting weak. He needed a new body, so he planted his soul inside of my father's daughter while she was in her mother's womb. A soul must be pure from evil in the afterlife because if not, the reincarnated body will still have visions of the Underworld. Naobi told King Baki to get rid of Meda when she was a baby but he said all babies were innocent. I knew this shit was going to come back in some way and that's why I made an agreement with him that our world would remain separate. No one from Anubi is supposed to come near this pack," he said and stood up.

"What my sons see, I can see, too, but only if I'm concerned. I knew you two were hiding something," he said and fixed his suit jacket. He looked at his gold watch with red ruby diamonds outlining the face.

"I have a meeting in a few and my car is downstairs waiting for me. I will handle everything from here on out. I will find a way to reach King Baki," he said and walked to the door.

"Akea," his deep voice called out when he turned around.

"Yes, Father," I answered.

"Make sure you tell Dayo about you and his daughter. I don't want it to go the same way it went with me and Izra. Tell him before he finds out. You will gain a father's respect more," he said and walked out.

"Damn his warlock! I wish that nigga could just be a beast," Kanye fussed and sat down on the couch.

"I guess our plans are off," I said and stood up.

"Our plans are not off. We have warrior blood that flows through our veins. Why must we sit back and let our father do everything? He has two sons that are willing to do anything to keep them evil muthafuckas from Anubi away from him and he won't let us. It's our time, Akea. This is a new beginning for the pack—us. We need to have our own history and it starts here. What can he do? Beat our asses with a belt like we are human kids?" he asked.

"He is onto us," I said.

"Get him off of us. You are the warlock," he spat. Kanye wanted me to go against our father.

Maybe I can break the rules a little bit, I thought.

Monifa

"Is everything okay?" I asked Baneet. I was laying across her bed while she cried her eyes out over Zaan.

"I cannot believe he said those things to me. I gave him my virginity," she cried.

"I know but let him have the connection to you. Male wolves are very sexual and will screw anything if there is not a connection. He doesn't feel what you feel and if you love him you should give him that connection. I still cannot believe you made him wear a muzzle during sex. I don't know if I want to call that animal cruelty or domestic violence," I said and she threw a pillow at me. A slight giggle slipped from her lips.

"I don't want to laugh at you," she said. Arya came into Baneet's bedroom with her house clothes on. She had a bowl of ice cream for her and Baneet. She didn't speak to me and I didn't speak to her. Maybe it was because of Kanye. The first female offspring is usually the one that mates with the next alpha male. In Arya's eyes, Kanye was supposed to be hers. In most packs, the two females tried to outdo each other to get the male to notice and make his pick. The gods beat her to it because I was the chosen one.

"I'm going to head home. Me and Kanye have a date tonight," I said. I hugged Baneet and Arya rolled her eyes.

"Is there a problem?" I asked Arya.

"No, little girl, there is no problem," she said.

"Girl?" I asked.

"I would've called you a beast but being as though you are a witch, too, I prefer to use girl. Witches are just humans that cast spells and live for eternity. You are not a beast," she said.

"And you are a hoe just like your mother. Don't think I haven't heard how your real mother used to sell her wolf pussy to the humans! I guess the apple doesn't fall too far from the tree, bitch!" I said and Baneet covered her mouth.

"Monifa, that was rude!" Baneet yelled at me.

"I stated facts," I spat and Arya stood up.

"Coming from the bitch who has the spirit of a demon whore inside of her. I remember Keora; she fucked Goon and she fucked Dayo. Why should the gods give you Kanye after you fucked his father and pack brother? It must be a spell that you casted on him just like how your mother casted one on Izra. We could've been sisters because Izra screwed my real mother under Adika's spell. I know this pack's history. I was here before your afterlife," she fussed. I slapped her in the face as hard as I could and she flew into the wall. She wanted to shift but Baneet grabbed her arm.

"Not in my room," Baneet said. Arya snatched away from her and charged into me. She slammed me on the floor and sat on top of me. Her sharp wolf nails slashed across my face. I punched her in the face and she fell over. I dragged her by the hair and threw her out of the window. The glass cut across her face and she landed in the backyard. I leaped out of the window and sat on top of her.

"Little girl? I will show you little girl!" I screamed and slapped her across the face again. She shifted underneath me and latched onto my arm with her sharp teeth. Her beast slung me into the house and my back snapped. I felt my body changing but not into a beast. I was changing into that other part of me—the part of me I felt when I was angry. My body floated up in the air and my hair grew into long, thick ropes. My hair moved around on the top of my head and a stronger energy surged through my body. The clouds darkened and the trees blew like a storm was coming. Blue lightning floated in the palm of my hands and my voice changed. I spoke in an ancient Egyptian language.

Who are you? I asked but it didn't respond. The blue balls of fire slammed into Arya's beast and she yelled out in pain. The ground cracked and a few trees fell over.

"STOP IT, MONIFA!" my mother yelled when she ran out of the house. Arya's beast laid on the ground, injured. My mother sent a bolt of electricity into my body. The energy I had in my body started to weaken me. I felt myself falling onto the ground...

****

When I woke up, I was in my condo. My mother came into the room with a cup of Elle's tea. I slowly sat up with my head throbbing.

"What happened?" I asked.

"Your witch is becoming stronger. You have Keora's witch and she was very powerful, even before she practiced dark magic. She studied all the ancient Egyptian spells. You have that inside of you," she said. I grabbed the hot tea and sipped on it and immediately my headache went away.

"What does Elle put in this stuff?" I asked and she laughed.

"I don't know but Anik is very upset that you used magic on Arya," she said and I shrugged my shoulders.

"She started with me. She wants Kanye and she can't have him. She seduced him before and I saw visions of it.

He was aroused for her and she was hot for him. I have his markings, not her, and it's not fair to me that I had to see that," I fussed.

"Arya is a tough one. When she first came into the pack, she was ten years old. She was taught to be promiscuous from a wolf named Sosa. He was teaching her how to seduce men. He owned an underground sex-slave ring," she said.

"Did you put a spell on my father so that he could sleep with another wolf? I asked.

"I wanted a pup. I lost a baby and Izra didn't know how to cope with it. I couldn't give birth, so I wanted him to impregnate another wolf so that we could raise the pup together. I just wanted to make him happy and I almost lost him. Promise me you will never put a spell on Kanye," she said.

"I promise. What was Keora really like?" I asked.

"Keora was everything. But after I thought about it, all she wanted was to be loved. Love turned her wicked and love cured her spirit. I cannot talk bad about her even after all of the chaos she caused because she gave me her soul. She didn't have to but she knew how badly I wanted a baby," she replied. The front door opened. Kanye's scent was strong—very strong.

"Let me get going. Rest up," my mother said before she disappeared. I got out of bed and he was in the kitchen, shirtless. My eyes roamed over his muscled and tatted back. He turned around with glowing blue eyes.

"You are finally up," he said.

"How long have I been asleep?" I asked.

"Three days. I got your school work on the table," he replied. His eyes roamed over my body and I felt the desire he had for me. He wanted me more than ever.

"You are spreading," he said referring to my hips. I walked over to him and pulled him into me.

"Let's take a shower," I said. He took his jeans, boxers, and socks off in the middle of the kitchen floor. His long, thick dick hung between his legs. I noticed the new tribal markings he had on his legs.

"When did you get those?" I asked.

"This morning. It didn't hurt as bad as the other ones did," he said. His body was perfectly sculpted and the markings added to it—he was beautiful. I headed for the shower and he followed behind me. He grabbed my butt and growled.

"Keep your hands to yourself," I said.

"I can't help it. I was thinking about you all day in school. I had to walk around with a hard-on and I scared the fuck out of Ms. Lupus when I walked into her class. She called the police and told them she thought I had a gun. I almost bit her head off. She thinks I'm gangbanging or something," he fussed.

"You sorta remind me of a gangbanger," I laughed.

"The police came and searched me. It was a female officer and when she felt all of that dick, she got aroused. Her scent wasn't a good one, though. It reminded me of a deer carcass," he said. Kanye was a jerk.

"Opposite of Arya's scent, huh?" I asked.

"What is that supposed to mean and why are we discussing her?" he asked.

"It's not supposed to mean anything. I just want to know," I said.

"If I tell you the truth about it, you won't like it," he replied. I rolled my eyes and stepped into the shower.

"Why are you mad, Monifa? I wasn't mad when you were fucking the human boy! I was supposed to be the only male to enter you. I had to come second to a punk-ass human," he complained.

"Are you telling me that I'm a whore?" I asked.

"What in the fuck is wrong with you? You know what, take your ass back to sleep. I'm taking a shower in the guest bathroom," he said. He tried to walk out of the bathroom and the door slammed in front of him. He turned the knob and it burned his hand.

"Crazy bitch!" he yelled out and I laughed. He punched a hole through the door and turned the knob from the other side.

"I'm leaving," he threatened.

"What?" I asked. I rinsed the soap off and stepped out. I grabbed a towel and he looked at me with anger-filled eyes. Kanye had a serious temper problem.

"I'm leaving is what I said. Have pups by yourself. Better yet, since you are the witch, create your own dick and fuck yourself with it," he fussed.

"Don't talk to me like this!" I yelled.

"You started it with me. I couldn't wait to get home to you and you want to question me about Arya's scent," he replied.

"You're only mad because I put you on the spot! You know you enjoyed her scent and you want to argue about it because you don't want to answer me."

"Okay, you want to know the truth? Fine! Her scent is delicate, the same as yours," he replied. I pushed passed him then headed to our bedroom. He followed me.

"How am I supposed to compete with that?" I asked.

"We are mates, therefore, it's not about competition," he replied.

"But we have not mated yet, so your nose is still wandering. Until we mate, you will be aroused by her. We are not permanent until you plant your seed inside of my womb. What if she gets to you first?" I asked.

"I'm not discussing this anymore," he said.

"I want to because I love you," I said. I was in love with Kanye before I knew he was my mate. I should've known then because everything he did bothered me. I was in denial at first because I didn't know what the feeling was until our souls connected spiritually. He didn't respond, he just stared at me.

"Don't answer that," I said and headed to my closet. I got dressed in a Nike sweat suit and a pair of Air Max's.

"I guess you think you are walking out of that door," he said.

"I can disappear in your face if I want to," I replied. I walked around him and he grabbed my arm.

"Where are you going?" he asked.

"To hunt," I replied and disappeared. I ended up across the street from a bar. I walked in and sat down. It was me and a few others sitting at the bar.

"Can I see your ID?" the middle-aged white man asked me.

I'm over twenty-one, pour me a drink, I said to him. He smiled at me. I was inside of his head but he wasn't aware that he was under my spell. He poured me a drink and placed it in front of me.

"It's on me," he said and went to wait on someone else. I was jealous of Arya and it was driving me crazy. It was a phase female wolves went through when it was time to mate. I was possessive but it was in my nature and there was nothing I could do about it.

"I'm surprised to see you here," a voice said from behind me. When I turned around, it was Yardi.

"I needed some air," I replied flatly. He sat down next to me.

"You smell good," he said and I laughed.

"Thank you. I'm trying out Amadi's new soap," I replied. He sniffed my neck and his nose tickled me.

"I missed you," he said.

"I'm not surprised. I tend to have that effect on the male species," I joked and he laughed.

"I miss your taste," he said and looked me in the eyes. Maybe I was buzzed from the straight Vodka I had, but Yardi was different. He was more attractive.

"Did you change your haircut?" I asked him.

"Yes, do you like it?" he asked. I looked at his tapered sides and the smooth waves that swirled around his head. His goatee was lined up perfectly. His body changed also; he was more sculptured.

"You look handsome. Who is the lucky female?" I asked. His hand slid between my legs.

"You are, it's always been you," he said.

Pull away, Monifa! Pull away! You are just horny because you are in heat and Vodka gets you aroused every time, I thought. A moan escaped my lips and his fingers caressed my bud through the thin material of the sweatpants I wore. I didn't have on any panties and my wetness seeped through my slit. My nipples hardened and

I started to sweat. I wanted him to stop but I couldn't. It felt like something was luring me in—a stronger presence.

"What are you doing?" I asked.

"Nothing, let's stand outside and talk," he said and stood up. I followed him outside and a bat flew over my head.

"I hate bats," I said and giggled. We walked into the parking lot and I leaned against his car.

"What do you want to talk about? I need to head home soon," I said. He unzipped my jacket and slid my bra up. He pulled my nipple into his mouth. I was in a trance and didn't question the sharp teeth that brushed across my nipple. His hand slid into my pants and his finger entered my pussy.

"OOHHHHHH," I moaned. I heard growling but I ignored it. I felt like Yardi had control over me. Blue eyes stared at me from the woods across the parking lot and even knowing that Kanye's beast was watching me, I still couldn't pull away. My body had an orgasm. The bat flew over my head again and landed on Yardi's shoulder. The bat's red eyes stared at me. It flew up above Yardi's head and turned into Osiris.

"Don't stop on my account," he said. Yardi's eyes turned red and his teeth sharpened—he was a vampire. I should've known he was something because I felt stuck around him and he never had me aroused before.

"You tricked me?" I asked and he pulled away from me. Kanye's beast stepped out of the woods followed by Zaan, Baneet, Chancy, and Akea. Wolf men came out of the bar and a few came out of the woods.

"They followed your scent," Yardi said floating around in the air.

"How does it feel to watch your mate pleasured by something you hate the most?" Osiris teased Kanye. Kanye's beast leaped up into the air but Osiris turned into a bat and flew off. Kanye growled at Yardi and Yardi turned into a wolf man. The rest of the pack charged into the wolf men. Yardi and Kanye were biting and clawing each other. Akea turned a few wolf men into ashes. I shifted and charged into Yardi but a wolf man grabbed my beast. I fought him off and sent an electrical bolt into his chest. More wolf men ran into the parking lot from out of the woods. Cars were sliding across the ground from fighting and the parking lot was filled with blood but we were outnumbered. Chancy ripped one wolf man in half and flung his lower body into the air. Zaan's beast was snapping necks and severing heads. Kanye's beast sank his teeth into Yardi's neck and I heard the sickening sound of flesh being ripped apart. A few minutes later, the wolf men laid across the parking lot, dead. Osiris came back and his bat was larger— it was almost the size of a man.

He came in and swooped up Yardi's body and flew away with him.

"Damn it!" Akea yelled out. We were weak from fighting and our magic wasn't as strong because our energy was overheated. Kanye's beast growled at me before it attacked me. His beast slammed me into a tree and his teeth sank into my shoulder. I bit him back but he couldn't feel it.

You betrayed me!

I didn't mean it! You are hurting me! I replied. Zaan, Chancy, and Baneet wrestled him off of me. He shifted into his human form and pain filled his eyes. His eyes watered.

"I almost killed you. Stay the hell away from me and I mean it! If you come near me, I'll rip your head off!" he yelled at me.

He shifted again and took off through the woods. Akea and Zaan followed him. Baneet and Chancy stayed with me. I shifted into human form and blood dripped from the wound he gave me. Seconds later, my skin pulled together.

Get on my back, Chancy said. I gripped her fur and pulled myself up onto her back. Baneet followed behind us as we disappeared further into the woods.

A few days later...

"For the last time, it was not your fault. Osiris had the same effect on me. It's something about vampires. They can get into our heads without reading our thoughts," Chancy fussed. We were in my living room discussing the night when Kanye's beast attacked me.

"He doesn't want me," I said.

"He's just mad. The jackass really has feelings. Poor guy, I actually felt sorry for him. He was really crushed," Baneet said.

"Don't remind me," I replied.

"You were set up. Yardi picked up your scent. I cannot believe that punk was turned into a hybrid," Chancy fussed.

"I should've had more control," I said.

"Damn it, Monifa. You are in heat. What control can you have over someone touching you? I'm not in heat and Osiris almost had my legs open before Akea stopped him. I could only imagine how aroused you were," Chancy said.

"I understand that but does Kanye?" I asked.

"He understands. He is just stubborn and arrogant. Maybe he just wants a reason to fuck Arya," Baneet said. She didn't mean any harm but it was a low blow.

"That was rude," Chancy said.

"I didn't mean it like that," Baneet said.

"Why would you say that, knowing Arya's scent attracts Kanye, too? I need a vacation because it's just too much. I thank the gods my nerd is a witch. I don't have to worry about Akea picking up scents," Chancy said and Baneet growled.

"But he was still in love with Sarah Baxter. You saw how he tried to rescue her from those wolf men," Baneet said.

"Why are you being a bitch?" I asked her.

"I'm not being a bitch but the both of you called me out on my relationship, remember? Sorry if it seems that way. I'm just being honest," she said and I rolled my eyes.

"Bitter bitches are always jealous when they are lonely," Chancy said.

"I'm not jealous. I want her to be with Kanye but I also think that our sister should be with him, too. Am I the only one who cares about Arya's feelings?" Baneet asked.

"I do care about Arya but the gods didn't pick her, they picked Monifa!" Chancy yelled.

"Arya said Adika cursed Kanye," Baneet said.

"Get out before I whip your ass. That's foolishness and you know it," Chancy spat.

"I just find it odd that the gods picked two wolves that never got along and still don't get along to be together and have pups," Baneet fussed.

"I find it odd that the gods didn't pick anyone for you! I cannot believe you listened to what Arya said about my mother! And for the record, I always loved Kanye! I loved him before I found out who he was to me. Arya just wants him for pleasure but I want him for eternity!" I yelled at her.

Baneet grabbed her purse and stormed out of my home. My love life was spiraling and so was my friendship. Baneet and Chancy were like my sisters and I wanted to cry because Baneet and I never argued.

"You can leave, too," I said to Chancy.

"I'm still your sister. That will never change," she said and grabbed my hand.

"Never," she said again. She kissed my forehead before she left out behind Baneet.

****

I waited outside of Kanye's class. He walked out with Daja and she was all smiles. When she saw me, she growled.

I'll come to your house again, I said.

Witch, she replied and walked off. Kanye walked passed me and I caught up to him.

"I'm sorry," I said and he chuckled.

"You stood there and let him give you pleasure in the front of my face. I think you did it because of Arya," he said.

"I couldn't pull away," I said.

"What if the next time Arya throws her pussy at me and I give you the same excuse. Will I get a pass?" he asked.

"It's not the same because you will be doing it out of spite. You are trying to hurt me and I wasn't trying to hurt you," I replied.

"I'll be by later to get my things. I'm going back to the mansion. I should've never left. Maybe you can mate with one of those horny-ass wolf men," he spat and walked off.

I wanted to burst into tears but I held it in. I zoned out in all of my classes for the remainder of the school day. When I got home, I laid across the couch. I hadn't been eating and I started to feel sick. I was very weak and my muscles ached. I started sweating and got up to get a pitcher of water. The door unlocked and it was Kanye. He walked in and headed straight to the bedroom. I laid across the couch and watched TV.

"Where is my jewelry?" he called out.

"In the trash just like the rest of your things," I lied. I made it disappear but it wasn't gone. It ended up in the trunk of my car. He stormed out of the bedroom and grabbed me by my shirt.

"Where are my things at, Monifa?" he asked and I pushed him away from me.

"I told you already," I spat.

"Okay, nigga. I'll just buy new shit then," he spat. His rage made me aroused. My hand slid up his pants leg and between his legs. He was aroused, too. I was dripping and my scent made his eyes turn. His teeth and nails sharpened.

"Fuck me, Kanye," I said. He snatched away from me and headed to the door. I appeared in front of the door. I unbuttoned my blouse and he stared at me.

"I don't want to," he said. I placed my hand inside of my panties and pulled it out. I rubbed my fingers across his lips and a deep growl slipped from him. His beast was fighting it. He grabbed me around my neck and his other hand ripped my bra off. He ripped off my leggings and thong. He rubbed between my slit and I moaned. I was dripping onto the floor. He sank his teeth into my breast and my eyes rolled upwards. I bit my lip and my sharp teeth drew blood. I needed him more than I needed air. My body was hot and I was trembling underneath his touch. I unzipped his pants and pulled them down along with his boxers. He turned me around and dug his nails in my scalp. He pulled my hair back and it caused me to arch my back. My sex was exposed and throbbing. His dick pierced through my tight opening without warning. He pulled my hair tighter and slammed into me. My feet raised off the floor and I scratched at the wall. He slammed into me again and I screamed out. One of his hands had my hair and the other hand was wrapped around the back of my neck. My pussy gripped him and he growled. He slammed into me over and over again until my essence was running continuously down my leg. I cried his name and he went harder. He was taking his frustrations out on me.

"I can't take it! It's too much," I moaned. He smacked my bottom and gripped both of my cheeks. He bent his legs and dug upwards inside of me. Pressure from him swelling filled my stomach.

"Shut up!" he growled and went faster and harder. I had another mind-blowing orgasm. The wall cracked and chips of paint fell onto us. He pulled out of me and turned me around. He picked me up and I straddled him. He lowered me down onto him and slid me up and down his shaft. His nails dug into my hips and I could barely hold on. He bounced me up and down his massive dick like I was a rag doll. He grunted and growled as sweat dripped down his chest. He lifted my right leg up and threw it over his arm. He was having his way with me, fucking me long and deep. He was savaging my pussy and I couldn't move because he was sending orgasms through my body back-to-back. He pulled out of me and laid me down on the floor. He lifted my legs up and sank his teeth into my clit. I squirted inside of his mouth. I gripped his head and grinded onto his lips. He slid his tongue in and out of me. His finger slid into my anus and I gasped.

I want it all! he said. A puddle formed underneath my bottom. He entered me in the other hole and I bit my lip. My nails dug into his shoulder and his fingers dug into my pussy.

Good ass! he groaned. He wasn't moving as fast because it was my first time trying anal sex. He didn't have all of himself inside of me but I still felt like I was being ripped apart. His fingers moved in and out of me and my bottom loosened up for him. I was leaking from both holes from being extremely aroused.

    GGGGGRRRRRRRRRRR! FUCK! I'M ABOUT TO BUST! he thought. His sharp teeth pierced through my breast and he started jerking. When he swelled inside of me, he bit his bottom lip and I felt his semen shoot inside me. My pussy gushed and dripped down my crack—I exploded. He fell on top of me and I couldn't move. I drifted off into a peaceful sleep...

    When I woke up hours later, I was in bed. My hair was still wet and my body was moisturized with Amadi's oil. Kanye gave me a bath but I didn't remember because I was asleep. I climbed out of bed and our home was empty. He left me and didn't wake me up to tell me he was leaving me again.

Kanye
The next day...

I didn't want to leave Monifa but I was somewhat still pissed off. I gave her passion because she asked for it but it didn't mean I was cool about what happened. It was my first time getting my feelings crushed—never mind, I take that back. I was crushed when she first started dating Yardi. She always talked about her dates with him to Chancy and Baneet around me, rubbing it in my face to get me to react.

I was in the back of a limo with Akea and my parents. We had another Beastly Treasure opening and we wore black and gold. My mother wore a long, black dress with a gold diamond choker. My father wore a black suit with a gold shirt underneath. Akea and I wore the same thing he did, but the only difference was that I didn't have a shirt on underneath my suit. My chest was bare with my tribal markings showing, a thick gold chain with red diamonds inside of it was draped around my neck.

"You just want to draw attention, don't you?" my mother asked and sipped her champagne.

"Leave him alone, Kanya. Kanye is just feeling himself at the moment," my father said and Akea chuckled.

"Who knows how many wolves that will be in heat in attendance tonight. The only attention he needs is from his mate," she said.

"It's not the clothes, beautiful, it's his scent, so let him wear what he wants. This is our event and if they don't approve of his image then so be it," my father said and she growled at him.

"Akea looks like a gentleman and Kanye looks like a rapper," she said.

"Again, Kanya. Leave it alone," he warned her. He kissed her cheek and she smiled.

"I will for now but I'm sending him a new wardrobe tomorrow," she said.

"I'm a twin. Can I at least be different? This is how people can tell us apart. If me and Akea dressed the same, how would you know who I am? I'll have to shift so that you could recognize me," I said.

"He has a point," Akea said. I grabbed the bottle of champagne and poured myself a glass. I gave the bottle to Akea and he looked at our parents.

"We are not old enough to drink," he said and my father laughed.

"Nigga, you keep waiting to be old enough and you will wait for eternity. Our age slowed when we turned eighteen. Get with it, bro, and besides, I told Ma that we got drunk the other night," I said and she chuckled.

"He blasted you, son," our father said to him.

"Stay in school and keep your grades up is all I'm expecting from the two of you. Your mother got a list of things," our father said and she smacked his arm.

When the limo stopped in front of the black, shiny building with huge windows, the door opened for us. We stepped out and onto the red carpet as the cameras flashed. Our father wrapped his arm around our mother's waist and she smiled for the cameras. They wanted a picture of me and Akea. I smiled and the women started blushing. I had gold caps over my fangs that matched my necklace. Another limo pulled up and Monifa stepped out—my heart stopped. Her dress was black and made of lace and the material was thin and looked like it was painted on her. I could see every curve she had. Her breasts sat up perfectly and she was braless. Her hair was jet black and it was styled in big loose curls like a mane. Her gold lipstick sparkled and the cameraman snapped a picture of her after she posed for him.

"She's beautiful, bro. Are you still mad at her?" Akea laughed.

Chancy stepped out of a limo wearing a black, lace cat suit and pointy heels. I didn't care to see what Baneet wore. Arya came out of nowhere and squeezed in between me and Akea. Her ass was pressed against my crouch area and her dress flew up, exposing her bare ass.

When the cameraman snapped a picture of us, Monifa laughed as she walked passed us.

That little witch! Arya thought. Arya wore a simple black dress with the back out. It dipped very low and I could see the two dimples above her butt. Our mother cut the ribbon in front of the doors and we walked into the building. Everyone was in awe because the inside of the building looked like a temple in Egypt. Big statues of pharaohs were lined up against the wall and the statues wore jewelry. There were showcases all over the room with ancient pieces displayed inside of them and some of them cost a few million.

"I would like everyone's attention," our mother said out loud. Every one stopped talking and watched her.

"Your mother is wearing the hell out of that dress," Zaan whispered.

"My father would've bit the hell out of you if he heard that," I said and he chuckled.

"Goon and I would like to dedicate all of this to our sons, Akea and Kanye, who turned into intelligent and handsome young men. This is a gift to the two of you," she said and the curtain behind her dropped. The name *A&K Jewels* was etched in the middle of the wall in front of us.

Bro, do I really have to interact with people? I asked Akea.

It will be fun but at least we can have our own fortune. This is sweet, bro, he replied. Everyone started clapping and we walked through the crowd. We hugged our parents and I kissed my mother on the cheek.

"Congrats, bro!" Zaan said and we shook hands.

"Don't be selling this jewelry on the street, either, like some crackhead," Chancy teased.

"Congrats," Baneet said to us. Monifa gave Akea a hug and she gave me a dry "Congrats" and walked off.

"This little nigga looks GQ," Dayo said when he walked over to me and I laughed.

"I learned it from you, big uncle," I said and playfully punched his arm.

"Aight, that's enough. You ain't a pup no more. You are like the Incredible Hulk now," he joked.

"Where was my invite?" a voice said from behind me. When I turned around, it was my grandmother, Naobi. She traveled the world a lot with her mate, Kumba. She had a home in Africa hidden in the jungle. She kept in touch but we didn't see her much. She said she had a lot of catching up to do with her mate for the years they lost with each other.

"Hey, Grandma," I said. She kissed my cheek then she kissed Akea's.

"You two are almost Goon's size," she said. My father told me she was thousands and thousands of years old but she didn't look over forty-five.

"I cannot believe how handsome the two of you are," she said.

"That's because I did all of the work," our father said and our mother blushed.

"He still says what he wants, I see," Naobi laughed. Everyone mingled in with each other but my father didn't look too happy.

"What's up with you?" I asked him.

"I haven't seen Kofi in twenty years. He is in Anubi and with the law, he must stay in Anubi," he said. I hadn't met Kofi but my father talked about him a lot. He referred to Kofi as his father, and on special events, his mood changed because he always wanted Kofi there.

"You want to wrestle?" I asked and he chuckled.

"And scare all of these humans?" he asked.

"Yeah, why not? Akea can zap their minds and make them forget," I joked and he patted my shoulder.

"Thanks, son, but I have to decline that offer. The last time we wrestled, your mother ignored me for two days and that's too long for my beast," he said.

"Come on, Father, I don't want to hear that, but can I ask you something?" I asked and we walked off to the side.

"Are you happy with our mother? Do you have the desire to give passion to other females?" I asked.

"No, but a lot of women throw themselves at me daily. I'm still a man and I do admire the structure of a woman, especially her curves and round bottom. When you mate, no one else can break that bond, but you have to be strong. If you hurt your mate, you end up hurting yourself. You feel what she feels. If you are cornered by two females in heat with lovely scents, always pick the one the gods chose for you. They know things that we don't know and Monifa has your markings, so that means she was made for you. You are a young beast and temptation will be there for other females. Before I met your mother, I slept with so many women that I could no longer get aroused. Temptation is only temporarily. You will feel the difference after you mate," he said.

"Can I borrow him for a second, Uncle Goon?" Arya asked when she walked over to us.

Remember what I said, he thought and walked off.

"You look very handsome tonight," she said with her eyes staring at my chest.

"You look beautiful yourself," I said and she blushed. Her scent tickled my nose and my dick pressed against my pants.

Stop, Kanye! Have some self-control, I thought.

If you need self-control around me then that just means I'm doing everything right, she thought.

"I have a soulmate," I said.

"I'm the female who is supposed to mate with the next alpha. The gods' choosing is a part of Egypt's tradition, which is passed down from your ancestors. My ancestors were Indians. Does that apply to me? No, it applies to Monifa but that doesn't have nothing to do with me. I'm going by what my ancestors stood by. I will have you, Kanye," she said. She pulled something out of her purse and stuck it inside of my pants pocket.

"My scent will change your mind," she said and walked off. I went inside of my pocket and pulled out a black thong and her scent was all over it. Arya wasn't playing fair. She knew I'd get aroused. When I turned around, Monifa was eyeing me.

I hope it will be worth it because I'm not fighting over someone who is supposed to be made for me. I'll send a gift for y'all's pups, she thought and walked out of the building. It was me and Akea's night, so our family was in attendance which was rare because everyone stayed busy running their own businesses. I should've been happy at that moment but I wasn't. I was feeling what Monifa was feeling and that was—feeling alone.

"Look at my two grandsons! Oh, God, they are so tall and strong," my other grandmother said. She was our human grandmother which was our mother's mother. She was in her sixties and had gray hair around her hair line. Our grandfather always questioned why my mother wasn't aging but deep down inside he knew what we were; he was in denial about it. Akea spent a lot of time with him but I didn't because he always called me the "bad twin".

"Hey, Grandma," I said and she squeezed my cheek.

"Hi, sweetie, sorry we are late. Your grandfather took the wrong exit. I don't know why that old fart still acts like he knows everything," she fussed.

"You look lovely tonight," I said and she smiled.

"You look edgy, a little too grown for your age but I guess since you don't age, it doesn't matter," she joked then she whispered to me.

"Kanya told me you have a mate. When is your mating ritual? I got to make sure I come here and spend the whole two months with Monifa when she gets pregnant. I always knew you two had it for each other, all you two did was fight and argue."

"It's on the next full moon and I'm pretty nervous about it," I said.

"Welcome to wolf hood," she joked. She pulled out a Ziploc bag from out of her purse and it was filled with homemade jerky that she made for me. It was bear meat, cow meat and deer meat mixed together.

"I swear, Grandma, you know just what I like," I said and she squeezed my cheek.

"Of course, I do. I have to give Kanya the recipe so she can make it when I die," she said. My heart dropped to the pit of my stomach.

"Die?" I asked.

"I'm getting old and eventually I will die. A human's lifespan comes and it goes," she said.

"Where is your shirt, Kanye and what on earth are you dressed like a gigolo for?" my grandfather asked me after he was finished talking to Akea.

"I'm a pimp with a bunch of hoes," I said and he grabbed his chest.

"No need to clutch your pearls, Grandpa, I was just kidding," I said.

"I've been telling Kanya for years that Goon and his fake brothers are bad examples of men," he fussed.

"Would you shut up, Jeffrey? Just shut up," Grandmother said.

"You always defend him and his father. They don't have any manners and talk to me any kind of way. Thank God Akea was brought up right," he said.

I can't wait until his human life expires, my father thought.

I don't think he is our grandfather. I think Grandma had another male on the side. I will not believe this human is kin to me, I replied and my father chuckled. My father walked over to us and hugged my grandmother. He held his hand out for my grandfather.

"How is everything, Mr. Williamson? I see that you are still full of life," my father said.

"I'm doing fine, very much. Not all of us have the luxury of worshipping the devil to remain youthful," grandfather spat.

"Like the old saying goes, black don't crack. You should know because your wife is still as beautiful as ever, if not more," my father said.

"Leave my wife out of it!" my grandfather yelled and I chuckled. He had the short man complex and he despised any man who was taller and bigger than him, especially when they gave compliments to his wife.

"Fair enough, there are appetizers and champagne coming around, help yourself, and we appreciate y'all coming," my father said before he walked away.

"I cannot believe you are acting this way at your grandsons' opening. You should be proud that they have something as great as this at a young age," my grandmother said to her husband.

"I will never be proud because I still don't understand their wealth. Where is this jewelry coming from? I've never seen anything like this before. I believe they are smuggling diamonds from Africa," he said and I wanted to knock him into the wall. I wanted a bond with my grandfather like the one he had with Akea but he always found a way to bad-talk me and my father.

"My father had very wealthy ancestors. Too bad the commercials are always showing starving kids from Africa and the diamond mines they die in, but you will not connect my ancestors to that," I said and I felt my blood boiling. I understood how my father felt because he got it worse from him. I loved my mother's father because I had to but I hated when he visited.

"Watch your mouth, young man! You need to have some respect for your elders. Your parents should've sent you to church with Akea," he said.

"Is everything okay over here?" my mother asked when she came over.

"I was just telling your son that he lacks manners. Perhaps, he should've been raised right. I think Akea should come back to New York with us. There are great schools and great jobs there. He would have a better life. He already has a room at the house, so all he needs to do is transfer schools," he said.

"Goon wants his sons in the same house, Father. Our family doesn't split and can you please keep the peace? If Goon hears you talking about this, it will ruin our special event. We've been down this road twenty years ago and it didn't end too well," my mother said.

"That's because you had sons by a man that I believe is a monster. His eyes turn blue and his teeth sharpen whenever he is angry. I'm telling you that it's not my imagination and I think Kanye has the same thing inside of him. That's why I wanted Kanye to come to church with Akea," he stressed.

"That is a bunch of nonsense, Jeffrey!" my grandmother shouted.

"It's not nonsense! These people are something and they turned our daughter into it. They still look the same from twenty years ago," he stressed.

"Everyone ages differently," my grandmother replied and he stormed away.

"The older he gets, the grumpier he becomes. I think the next time he should stay home. I will call him more often but I don't want him around Kanye because all he does is belittle him. Kanye isn't a baby anymore but he is still my baby and I will protect him forever; and if it means I have to protect him from my own father, I will do so," my mother said.

"I'm divorcing your father," my grandmother replied and my mother covered her mouth. I was shocked myself.

"This is just too much for me," my mother replied.

"I know, honey, and I was going to tell you later, but we've been having issues since the moment you had your boys. It drove him crazy and as bad as I wanted to tell him what you all were, I couldn't. It would've killed him and I'm trying to spare him, but I cannot do it anymore," she said sadly.

I walked away so that my mother could talk to her mother in private. I wasn't in the mood to be around anyone so I walked outside to the side of the building to smoke a blunt. It bothered me deep down inside how my grandfather made me feel. Every time he came around, I felt like a monster. I felt like my mother deserved a better life because, at times, I knew she missed being a human before she met my father. The only person who understood how I really felt was my father because he felt the same way, too. I wondered if Monifa felt pressured from the gods the same way my mother did. I remembered an argument between my parents years ago when I was ten years old. It was the first time I shifted...

"I don't like seeing him like this!" my mother cried. I was in the woods with my mother and the rest of the pack. I laid on a blanket sick and my body was overheated. My stomach hurt and it felt like I was being ripped apart. I also felt like I was burning and I was going to explode.

"It hurts, Father! Make it go away!" I cried and my arm snapped. Pain filled his eyes because he knew there wasn't anything he could've done for me. It was a part of

my life and who I was. A howl escaped my throat and my mother burst into tears.

"He is just a baby! Look at him! I can't stand it!" she screamed.

"What do you want me to do, Kanya? He is a werewolf and we knew this day was coming!" my father yelled at her. It was my first time hearing them argue that way.

"I wish you were human. I wish I didn't have this shit in me. Look at what it's doing to our pup. I can't deal with it. All I wanted was a human baby that didn't have to go through this. I wish he was like Akea," she said and my father growled at her. My bones snapped again and blood trickled from my skin as tiny gold and black hairs pierced through my skin like needles. The full moon came from behind the clouds and that's when I was introduced to my beast. My body was no longer that of a ten-year-old boy— I was a wolf.

I slept for two days after that and when I woke up, I had a craving to hunt for blood. I looked around the house for my father but he wasn't there. I went into the kitchen and asked my mother where he was but she didn't know.

"You said those mean things to Father. What if he never comes back?" I asked.

"He will come back," she said while she made Akea a sandwich. Akea sat at the kitchen table, reading a book. When I walked passed him, I knocked his book onto the floor.

"Why did you do that? Pick it up, Kanye, and do it now or else," our mother spat at me.

"You said you wished I was like him! I'm like Father and you don't like us," I said and I felt myself changing.

"That's not what I meant, so pick up the book or else you will be punished! No video games for you for a week!" she yelled. I ran out of house and through the woods. I roamed around the woods for hours until I picked up my father's scent. I followed his scent a few miles away. When I found him, he was sitting on a rock by a lake. His shoulders were slumped and he didn't seem like my father. My father was always a strong alpha male and never showed weakness. I placed my hand on his shoulder and he looked at me with tear-filled eyes.

"What happened, Dad?" I asked and he hugged me. When he released me, he wiped away his tears.

"I wished you were human, too, because this beast that we have takes a lot from us. It makes us mad, it makes you feel lost, and it makes you want to kill anything that betrays you. You can try to control it but beasts are stronger so they control us. I know this is what I am but *seeing you shift for the first time tugged at me, and in that moment I hated myself more than I ever did," he said.*

"I don't hate you, Father. I will never hate you," I replied and he chuckled.

"That's a good thing to know, son," he said.

"I didn't know beasts cry," I said.

"Anything with a heart will eventually cry, Kanye. Beasts weep alone. I didn't understand it at first until I met your mother. I cried for the very first time because I had gotten so angry with her I almost killed her. She was scared of me and I know that she still is, so when she makes me mad or if we argue, I stay away because that part of me doesn't show remorse all of the time," he said.

"She makes me mad when she says mean things to you," I said.

"When you get older and you meet your mate, you will experience the same thing. Me and your mother love each other, we just don't always agree on the same things," he said and stood up.

"I'm going to walk you home and when you get in the house, you will eat dinner, shower, and go to bed. I saw what you said to your mother and you are grounded for that. No video games for a week," he said.

"Come on, Dad. That's not fair, I was sticking up for you," I said.

"Not when it comes to your mother, you don't. I will worry about that, now let's go," he said. He walked me home but he didn't come in...

I learned a valuable lesson that day; love wasn't easy and neither was being a beast. Not everyone was going to accept us. But I knew who accepted it and I had to make things right because I loved her.

Two days later...

After doing a lot of thinking in my room back at the mansion, I decided to go back home. I knocked on the door and she didn't open it. I heard giggling coming from down the hall in the building and it was Monifa, but she wasn't alone. She was with an older guy who looked to been in his mid-twenties.

"Okay, Rocky. I will see you later and thanks again," she said. She walked away and he watched her ass. I heard the lustful thoughts he had of her.

"Aye, is there a fucking problem with your eyes?" I asked him and he scurried off.

"Who was that clown?" I asked when she walked to the door.

"He's a tutor at school. I've been in a funk lately and my work was piling up, so he helped me so I wouldn't fail this semester. We were at the coffee shop around the corner. Wait a minute, why am I explaining myself to you?" she asked.

"Because I'm your man," I said and she laughed.

"Go home, Kanye," she said and unlocked the door. She tried to close it in my face but I pushed it open.

"I am home," I replied.

"You can't barge your way back in whenever you feel like it!" she spat.

"I'm not trying to. I want to talk to you," I replied.

"Get to talking and you've got five minutes," she said.

"Okay, baby mama," I said and she blushed.

"Asshole." She laughed.

"I know I can be but damn I'm a nigga with flaws and we are soulmates because you can tolerate it," I said. I went inside of my pants pocket and pulled out a necklace. The diamond was so pure that it was clear.

"Is that the necklace Yardi gave me?" she asked.

"I stole it to get a real diamond put inside of it," I replied. She turned around and pulled her hair up. I put the necklace around her neck.

"It's pretty," she said. I caressed her face and she blushed.

"Just like you," I replied. She kissed my lips and I picked her up. I kissed her back and she wrapped her arms around my neck.

"Let's go out and celebrate," she said.

"You just like partying," I replied.

****

Monifa stood in front of me, shaking her ass in my face. I sank my teeth into her cheek. She was drunk and so was I. The loud rap music blared through the speakers inside the club. Her body moved like a snake.

"Monifa is on something, bro," Zaan said and she growled at him.

"Let's dance, Akea," Chancy said. Me and Zaan fell over in laughter.

"What's funny?" Akea asked.

"I don't know why that nigga is laughing but what do you know about ass shaking?" Zaan asked Akea.

"Ask Chancy what I know and she can tell you better," Akea replied.

"Pick your face up, nigga," I said to Zaan and he chuckled.

"Akea knows what to do with all of this beast," Chancy bragged and Akea smiled. Monifa sat down on my lap. She put her lips over the blunt I was smoking and I blew smoke into her mouth. She coughed and I patted her back.

"You better use some of that magic, beautiful. You are scaring me. Don't smoke and drink shit else," I said and she fell out into a fit of giggles.

"Monifa is done," Zaan said.

"She higher than Anubi," I said and Monifa laughed harder. She slapped my arm and her pupils turned jet black and then they turned yellow.

"I feel so freakin' good right now! I can go for Kanye's big, juicy and beautiful d—" she said as I covered her mouth. Akea pushed the liquor bottle over to Chancy and gave her a blunt.

"What do you want me to do? I don't smoke," Chancy said and rolled her eyes.

"He wants you to get freaky like Monifa's hot ass. He is trying to send you into heat," I joked with Chancy.

"I don't need that to get hot. I just take it from him," she said arrogantly.

"You and your sister just want to control muthafuckas. You raping my brother while your sister is treating Zaan like Kojo," I said and Akea laughed. Chancy tried to be mad at me but she ended up laughing, too.

"Ugh, I can't stand you!" Chancy said.

"Baneet is having the time of her life. Chancy, why don't you teach your sister how to dance? She's dancing like bad magic got ahold of her. I ain't never seen no shit like that before," I said and Chancy growled. The pack knew whenever I smoked or drank, I joked a lot.

"Go to hell, Kanye," she said. Zaan looked at Baneet and she was dancing with a guy she met at the club. She was trying to make Zaan jealous but he was laughing at her.

"You really don't care?" I asked him and he shrugged his shoulders.

"I do but she tries to run our relationship and I'm the one that's slinging all the heavy meat," he said.

"We need to figure out what Osiris been up to. Him and his hybrids are too quiet like they are brewing something. Do you think we killed all of them that night in the parking lot?" Akea asked.

"No, I believe he is up to something but he's hiding right now. We have to look for him," I said.

"I'm down," Chancy said.

"I think us males should do this alone," Akea said.

"I can hang with the best of them," she replied.

"I'm in," Monifa slurred and I ignored her. Baneet came back to our VIP section and she flopped down on the couch, exhausted from dancing. She poured herself a glass of champagne.

"I'm having a blast," she said.

"A blast doing what? And what are you tired for? You weren't doing nothing," I replied.

"I'm having a blast moving on with my life to be more specific. I forgot potheads don't have much brain cells," Baneet replied.

"I'm happy for you," Zaan said to her.

"This is why I didn't want to come, Chancy. Zaan has to be a dick about everything," she fussed.

"What are you talking about? I'm glad you are having fun is all I said," Zaan replied.

"I'm floating on the clouds, sshhhhhh," Monifa said and laughed.

"I need to use the bathroom," I said and got up. When I walked into the bathroom, I smelled blood. A man was in the corner of the bathroom kicking his feet while another man sucked on his neck. The vampire looked at me with red, glowing eyes. His face formed into a wolf face and he burst out of his clothes turning into a wolf man.

"Damn, you are ugly," I said. It charged into me and I grabbed him by the neck. I slammed him into the wall and he tried to bite me. I slammed him again and he scratched my face. My nails sharpened and it pierced through its neck. Blood squirted onto the walls and my teeth sharpened. I clamped down into his neck and ripped his throat out. I dropped him on the floor next to the man he was feeding on.

"Damn it, I just got these Timbs," I said when I saw the blood all over them. When I turned around, Osiris was looking at me.

"I came here to do business and like always you ruined it. I'm fascinated by you. By the way, you just killed a hybrid without shifting into a beast. You are a great warrior," he said hanging upside down from the ceiling.

"Nigga, you act just like a bitch. I mean what man is comfortable with putting his mouth on another man's neck to suck his blood? I wonder if you leave hickeys," I said and his eyes glowed.

"I wonder if Yardi left one on your mate. She was so wet that even I could smell it," he replied and fell to the floor, landing on his feet. He stood up and brushed his shirt off. I charged into him and slammed him into the stall. The toilet cracked in half and a pipe burst. I wanted to kill him. He punched me but I didn't feel it. I head-butted him and he fell onto the floor. I grabbed the back of his neck and slammed him on the floor and the tile cracked. He stuck a needle inside of my leg and it burned my skin. My body went into shock and I fell onto the floor. Akea appeared in the bathroom and Osiris turned into a bat. He flew into the vent in the ceiling.

"It burns!" I growled. My heart was slowing down and I saw another world. A world where vampires fed on life in a dark place. I saw a glimpse of the Underworld.

"He poisoned you with his blood," Akea said. My body convulsed and Akea cut his arm and held it over my mouth.

"Drink my blood, so it can slow it down! Our blood together should overpower the poison," he said. He put his wrist over my mouth and I sucked on the blood that dripped from him. I howled and then everything went black...

You will come to me, soon. Your soul cannot fight me because I have the greater power! the voice said to me, but I couldn't wake up. I was trapped inside of something, like a small place filled with darkness.

Let me out! I yelled and it laughed.

Fight your way out, and if you can, your soul will be free; but if you can't, your soul will belong to me, it said.

Osiris

"You did good," Meda said to me because I gave Kanye my blood.

"How are my parents doing?" I asked.

She showed me her globe and I looked at my parents. They were in Anubi, stuck inside of a glass box.

"I did everything you wanted me to do and you killed them anyway," I said.

"They are not dead, just sleeping because I know that Naobi and her son, Goon, will try to find a way to get in touch with them. Everyone in Anubi is asleep until this blows over. I don't want any disturbances," she replied.

She walked around the place I called home with her long, gold silk robe dragging the floor. Her pitch-black slanted eyes stared at me.

"How do you feel about Chancy? We need a female sacrifice for all of this to be completed. I want her to give birth to Ammon's spirit after we get Goon's blood. A feisty female with a warrior heart will be great for Ammon's reincarnation," she said.

"She stays out of it! This is not my fight! It is your fight, bitch. I have nothing against them and you made me into this evil bloodsucking immortal!" I spat. She pulled out a necklace from underneath her robe. It was a stone with cloudy smoke inside of it.

"This is your beast's soul. You will do what I say until everything is finished... I have a surprise for you," she said. Two naked girls appeared in front of me. I recognized them from Anubi. They were servants.

"What are they doing here?" I asked.

"Do you want to know where they really came from? Those servants are from my spells. I created them because I knew this day was coming. I've been planning this for a while now. They are witches that can shift into beasts. The wolf men are not as strong as I thought they were going to be. All they do is kill and be killed. This is my last plan and it'd better work. Monifa is stronger than what she knows. You will need the help," Meda replied.

"We are here to service you, my prince," one of the witches said and I walked away.

****

The next night...

I walked through a dark bat cave with the two witches behind me. The witches wore hooded capes over their heads. The bats swarmed around me like a tornado twist.

"You are their master. Learn how to control them," Jutu said. Her sister didn't talk and her name was Fiti. They were both beautiful ebony women but darkness lurked their hearts because of Meda. I walked further down into the cave and Yardi's body lay on a sheet. I gave him more of my blood so that he wouldn't die. Kanye caused him to lose a lot of blood.

Yardi sat up and looked around.

"Glad to see you awake. You've been asleep for days," I said.

"What the fuck are you doing to me?" he asked.

"Using you to get what I want and you will get what you want. I want Kanye's father dead and you want wealth, we can help each other," I said.

"Who are they?" he asked talking about the witches.

"Friends from back home. They will help you carry out my request," I said. I sat on the chair that stood in the middle of the cave. Juta made fire appear on the torches that sat on each side of the chair. One of the bats flew toward me and perched on my shoulder.

"He's the chosen one. He will be your eyes at night and what he sees, you will see. He will be a spy for you. Let him drink your blood so he can connect to you," Juta said. I held my arm out and the bat crawled down my arm. I lifted up my sleeve and exposed my wrist. Its sharp fangs pierced through my wrist and it drank my blood.

"Come, we have work to do," Juta said to Yardi. He followed the witches out of the cave. I thought about Chancy and I wished that I met her when my life was pure. There was something about her that I couldn't let go.

Go find her, I thought and the bat flew away. I sat and waited for an hour until a vision came through of her. Chancy was with Akea in the woods behind their house. He lay on top of her and she stared into his eyes. She undressed for him and his hand passionately slid up her leg while he kissed her—he loved her. I banged my hand on the arm of my chair as I watched him make love to her. Her body trembled from his strokes because he was planted deeply inside of her. A tear of passion slid from her eye as he moved in and out of her.

How do you kill a warlock? I thought.

Akea

I jumped up and out of bed because I had another dream. In my dream, Chancy's eyes were red and my blood dripped from her mouth. In that dream her stomach was swollen with our child but our child was dead.

"What's the matter?" Chancy asked when she sat up. After we made love in the woods, I snuck into her room. She touched my arm and I snatched away from her.

"What is going on with you? Why are you crying?" she asked me.

"It was real. My dream was so real. My visions are telling me something," I said.

"I'm not going near Osiris. I changed my whole schedule in school just in case he comes back to school. I'm with you," she said. I wiped my tears away. In my dream, I was crying for her because she chose Osiris over me. She chose him over me while carrying my seed inside of her womb. Osiris's blood flowed through her veins and inside of my unborn child because he gave her his blood to drink.

"I don't know. I just need some space," I said and crawled out of her bed. I pulled up my pants and she climbed out of bed behind me, naked.

"What about me and my feelings?" she asked.

"In my dream, Osiris had an army full of vampires. Osiris fell in love with you. This is no longer about my father. This is going to be about you. He will sacrifice his home and his world to get you. I saw that in my vision. He will sacrifice his parents to gain more power. He will completely give his soul to a demon and he will not be Osiris anymore," I replied.

"You are scaring me," she said.

"I think we need to go to Anubi to get to the bottom of this," I replied.

"How are we going to get there?" she asked.

"I don't know but I will have to figure it out. I don't know how much longer I can block these thoughts of Osiris from my father," I said and I felt my head throbbing. At that moment, I regretted listening to Kanye when he told me to make sure Father didn't find out what we were up to.

"I will come with you," she said.

"I don't know if that's a good idea. I don't want your father to blame me if something happens to you. I can take the heat but I don't want you to," I replied.

"I'm with you every step of the way. You are not leaving me here. I want to protect you, too," she said. I kissed her forehead.

"I'm going to shower and get dressed. Meet me downstairs in an hour," I said and disappeared into my room. When I got out of the shower, I got dressed. I walked out of my room and Ula was standing by the stairs.

"Good morning, Akea," she said and a snake slithered around her arm.

"Don't worry, all snakes are not poisonous," she said and it disappeared.

"I did my research on vampires and it seems to me they are very spontaneous immortals," she said. We teleported into the inside of her sanctuary. It was a room where witches practiced and studied spells. She sat down across from me and lit a few candles. She chanted and her spell book opened.

"This vampire harbors the soul of a demon. The demon's name is Set. It's an evil god of the night from Ancient Egypt. His master is Seth, which is the god of the Underworld from Ancient Egypt. Set drinks blood to take the souls. Vampires are dead immortals because Seth harbors all their souls. This vampire collects the souls for Seth. Seth will become stronger and his presence will be strong enough to walk the earth. Seth will enter the body of his strongest vampire. When Osiris becomes stronger, Seth will take place of his body and impregnate a female so that his offspring can walk on Earth—a demon disguised as a human. His offspring will be a born vampire. The demon spirit, Set, which is Osiris now, will turn into a bat and wait for hundreds of years to get inside of another body before the blood moon," she said.

"Osiris is Set now but will become Seth? I had a vision of that. It looked like Osiris but it wasn't Osiris," I said and she nodded her head.

"Yes, Set is testing out Osiris for his master Seth. Once Seth is satisfied, he will take over Osiris's body. Seems like your vision is going to become true because our visions are predicting our future," she said.

"The baby Chancy was pregnant with was my baby," I said.

"It will be owned by a demon if the baby is inside of the womb of a vampire," she said.

"This is some satanic shit," I spat.

"When there is good, there is evil. You have the Gods of Egypt in the skies and you have the Gods of Hell in the Underworld," she said.

"We need to stop it," I said.

"You can't kill Seth because he is already dead. You can only get rid of his puppets to take away his source. He will weaken without his worker, Set," she said.

"How do you kill a vampire?" I asked.

"You can't kill something that's dead but if you burn it, its soul will go back to hell," she said and she turned her book around.

"This is the blood moon. When this moon rises, the vampires will feed on anyone with a pulse sending all the souls to Seth. It's a big night for him during the blood moon with a woman sacrifice," she said.

"The blood moon is in three nights," I replied.

"You will warn the pack. You need your father for this, Akea. You need to gather the werewolves from different packs and come together because every few minutes, a new vampire is born," she said.

"This is too much," I said and she chuckled.

"Welcome to adulthood. For centuries immortals clashed with other immortals. Even humans experience things of that nature. Different countries go to war because of terrorist attacks. You will only have peace when you die," she said. I stood up.

"You and Kanye are a strong pair," she said.

"I need to become a beast. Using my energy weakens me after a while but a beast never weakens," I said.

"You are a beast. Your brother is a part of you and you are a part of him. Two of the greatest powers are separated but it's up to the bond that you two have to become one. Your father knows what you two are capable of. He knows that you two are one in the same and it was important to him that you two share the gift with each other," she said.

"I'm lost," I replied and she rolled her eyes.

"For you to be on the Dean's List sometimes you don't have a clue. Your father wanted you to figure it out on your own but I guess I have to tell since you need it. You have the ability to enter Kanye's body and his beast has the ability to feed off your magic," she said.

"Get inside of him?" I asked.

"Inside of his beast. You are each other's missing links," she said.

"I need the spell," I said and she laughed.

"It's not a spell you use for it, Akea. It's the love between brothers. You have to dig deep within yourself but the energy is there," she said.

"Thanks, Ula," I said and turned around to walk out of her room. She called after me.

"When a witch does a favor for you, you do a favor for them," she said.

"Damn you old witches," I spat and a snake slithered around her.

"Watch it, nerd. All I want is that necklace inside of your store. The blue diamond one. It'll look good with the blue pumps I just bought," she said.

"Aight," I said.

****

"Where is Kanye?" I asked Monifa when Chancy and I walked into their home.

"In the shower, is everything okay?" she asked.

"The blood moon is in three days," I said.

"The blood moon, meaning the moon when the demon from hell walks the earth after it has enough souls?" she asked.

"How do you know?" I asked.

"I didn't know it just came out," she said.

"Keora's soul is allowing you to see things," I said. Kanye came out of the bathroom with a towel wrapped around his waist. He didn't remember much of the fight between him and Osiris after Osiris injected his blood inside of him. Kanye blacked out on the bathroom floor at the club that night for a few minutes. When he woke up, his eyes looked empty. Something was wrong with my brother and I was afraid to tell our father.

"Are you okay, bro?" I asked.

"I'm cool," he said and rubbed his head.

"Are you sure?" I asked.

"Bro, I said I'm fucking cool!" he said and banged his fist on the table. The table snapped in half and his eyes glowed.

"I don't think you are, Kanye. Last night you didn't want to touch me and you never deny my scent," Monifa said.

"I don't always want to fuck, Monifa. Is that okay with you? Can I have some peace sometimes?" he spat.

Something is going on, Akea, she said. I walked over to my brother and sat down next to him. I grabbed his hand and let his energy travel into my body. I saw visions of a dark shadow with red eyes. It was trying to feed off Kanye's soul.

"What's that face for?" Monifa asked.

"Kanye's soul is struggling to not go to the other side. He's fighting it but it's trying to pull him in. My blood wasn't strong enough to save him completely just strong enough to keep him from turning into a vampire," I said. Monifa gasped and tears fell from her eyes.

"What if his beast starts to weaken and can't fight it?" she asked.

"I don't know," I said.

"I'm calling your father," Monifa said and went into the room. Kanye sat still on the couch and stared at the wall. His eyes turned red then they turned blue.

"I apologize for every fucked up thing I said to you, bro. I love you and I just want you to know that before it takes me," he said.

"It's not going to take you, stop saying stupid shit!" I said, getting pissed off.

"When you leave, take Monifa with you. I don't want to mate with her knowing I'm not pure. I don't want to give this shit to her or my pups," he said.

"Stop talking like that!" Monifa screamed when she came out of the room. She hugged him and he just stared at the wall. Kanye was slowly losing his soul.

****

An hour later...

We all sat inside of the living room at the mansion. My father paced back and forth, seething.

"Calm down, Goon!" my mother shouted and he a punched a large hole inside the wall.

"I can't calm down! Akea used his magic against me and blocked me away from their thoughts. Look at Kanye! Look at him, Kanya, and tell me what you see. My got damn son is a demon, a fucking demon!" my father said. Kanye sat in the chair with his eyes turning red and switching to blue.

"Three fucking days and it will have his soul. That is not enough time. None of us can save him at this point," he said.

"We need to contact someone from Anubi," Elle said.

"Anubi's portal is closed and I can't contact anyone. I should've killed everyone there twenty years ago. Their problems always come here and to us," my father fussed. He kneeled down in front of Kanye and hugged him. He squeezed him tightly.

"Fight, Kanye! Fight it!" he said to him. My mother burst into tears. My father sobbed because there was nothing we could do. Monifa fell out onto the floor and screamed and everyone in the pack had teary eyes. It felt worse than him dying because we could see his soul slowly slipping away from him.

Monifa
A few hours later...

I sat in the woods at the lake where Kanye and I shared our first intimate moment. I held onto my necklace and cried. I just wanted everything to go back to the way it was, but that would've required me to practice black magic.

"What would Keora do?" I asked myself because I wanted her to speak to me.

"Answer me, damn it! I need you!" I cried out. The trees rustled and a breeze swept over the lake. I gasped when I saw the image before me. Her walk was seductive and her long locks dragged across the lake. The woman had pretty almond-shaped eyes and she was topless, but her hair covered her breasts. She had a piercing in her cheek with a tooth that belonged to an animal. She stood before me and my heart skipped a beat. I was scared to breathe.

"Who are you?" I asked.

"You called on me, but don't be scared. I'm not really standing in front of you. It's all a vision," she said and she sat down next to me.

"I need your help," I said and her black eyes looked at me.

"I am you. Only you can help yourself," she said.

"I want to practice black magic to save Kanye. Black magic is the only way to connect to the Underworld," I said.

"If you sell your soul, it will be hard to get it back," she answered.

"I don't care," I replied.

"I won't tell you. You have to dig down into your soul to figure out who you really are. You have everything I had. Naobi created me and Adika for specific reasons and that was to defeat the demons. I could shift into anyone I wanted to and your mother could shift into any animal she wanted to. You can do that. That's the key," she said.

"Shift into someone else?" I asked.

"To defeat the enemy, you have to get closer to the enemy. You don't need a spell, just let that side of you speak to you and it will happen," she said and disappeared. I headed home.

****

I stood in a mirror and looked at myself.

"Okay, Monifa, you can do this," I said. I closed my eyes and relaxed my body until a warm feeling flowed through my veins. I let my body take me places it had never been. I always felt like I was being restricted from something, like there was a locked door and I couldn't get in. The curtains blew and I heard the windows inside of my home breaking. I knew it was the energy from my body and it was unlocking that door that I could never get into. I heard the bedroom door open and slam and shut. Things flew across my room and my building shook like an earthquake. The glass in front of me shattered and flew into my face. The electricity traveled to my brain and I collapsed...

I woke up on the floor the next morning to the sounds of birds chirping. My head was pounding. I looked around my home and it was a mess. Glass was everywhere. I stood up and walked into the bathroom and a lock fell into my face.

"What the hell happened to my hair?" I asked myself. I had long, skinny dreadlocks that reached down passed my hips. I looked at my nails and they were long and pointy and painted black. I rushed to the cracked mirror on the medicine cabinet to look at myself. I looked the same but my hair was different and my cheekbones were higher. I stared at myself and then my face changed into someone else's. I focused on my image in the mirror and seconds later I turned into Chancy.

"This is freaking insane! Keora, I have to give it to you. You were a bad bitch, I mean witch," I said.

****

Later on at the pack's mansion...

"What happened to your hair?" Anik, the twins Baneet and Chancy's mother asked me.

"It's hard to explain," I said. Arya came into the kitchen with a glass of water in her hand. She rolled her eyes at me.

"What happened between the two of you?" Anik asked.

"She's jealous because Kanye wanted me first," Arya said.

"Who cares if he wanted you first, I have him now and forever. I will give everything up for him to be normal again. Can you see yourself doing that or do you just want to fuck him?" I asked and Anik gasped.

"The language, Monifa," she said.

"The nerve of this tramp that's standing in front of me. I almost went off the deep end last night to save

Kanye. He is my life, and the sooner you realize that, the better. Don't take me to that dark place, Arya. I will go there with not one ounce of regret. Stay the hell away from him!" I yelled at her. With Kanye in the state he was in, I didn't trust him around her. I walked out of the kitchen and up the stairs, down the long hallway. I opened up his room door and he was lifting weights on his weight bench. He sat up and wiped the sweat off his forehead.

"I think you should be home. I know the pack wants you here but I think you will be safer at home with me," I said.

"I don't answer to no one," he said and stood up. He towered over me and stared down into my eyes. He didn't even notice that my hair was different and his eyes didn't have the same passion it once held for me. Arya walked passed his room and he growled. She was teasing him and taunting him with her scent.

"This is not you, Kanye. You wouldn't disrespect me this way," I said and he chuckled.

"Stop bitching, Monifa. It's just pussy," he said and dropped his basketball shorts. He stood in front of me naked with his erection pointing at me.

"Do you want to take a shower?" he asked with red eyes staring at me. I backed away from him and he laughed.

"Just leave a nigga hanging? That bitch down the hall would've been on her knees by now," he said.

"This is not Kanye talking," I said and walked away from him. He grabbed me by the back of my neck and pressed my body, face down, against the wall.

"Stop it!" I said as his hands roamed over my body.

"Are you denying me of what belongs to me?" he asked. He sniffed the air.

"I can smell your arousal," he said into my ear. He turned me around and pinned my arms against the wall above my head.

"My body naturally responds to you. But this thing that is latching on to you will not have me," I said. He sucked on my neck and his teeth grazed my skin. A moan escaped my lips and I wanted to pull away but I couldn't. His touch felt the same and my body yearned for him, but it wasn't him. He pressed his naked body against mine and bit my bottom lip. His hand slid into my pants and he rubbed my swollen bud. I couldn't deny the hold he had on me and I became putty in his hands. He slammed his door shut and pulled me down onto the floor. Seconds later, I was naked and he was buried between my legs. The way he licked between my wet slit was just like Kanye. He pushed my legs up and covered my pussy with his mouth. He sucked harder on my pussy and I started throbbing. My clit jumped and I dug my nails into his back.

"Oh God, Kanye, I love you so much!" I cried and he sucked harder. His long tongue slid into my tight, dripping hole and his sharp canines brushed across my clit. I was dripping onto the floor and I felt wetness underneath my body. My body was getting hot and a cramp formed in my lower stomach as Kanye's mouth took me places. He threw my legs over his shoulder and my lower half was raised off the floor. He held me up underneath my ass and continued to feast between my legs. I grabbed my breasts, squeezing them while humping his face.

"Grrrrrrrrrr," he lustfully growled. I was dripping and my essence ran up my back. I screamed louder and my legs shook from having another orgasm. I wanted him inside of me.

"Fuck me, Kanye! Please, I need it!" I begged and he eased me down. He turned me over onto my stomach and spread my ass cheeks. He stuck his nose in my pussy from the back and licked from my slit to my crack. My sharp nails scratched his floor and he laid his heavy body on top of mine. He bit my shoulder and slid his dick into my tight opening.

"UHHHHHHHHHH," I moaned when I felt him in my stomach, but seconds later he pulled out of me. I turned around and sat up and he was sitting on the edge of his bed.

"I can't do this, Monifa. I don't want it to feel how you feel inside. I don't want to share you with it," he said sadly. He looked at me and grabbed my hair. He traced his thumb across my lips.

"I like your hair like this. You always look good to me, even when your hair is all over your head," he said and a tear fell from my eye.

"Kill me. It will leave my soul alone if you burn me," he said.

"What?" I asked.

"My soul cannot fight it anymore. There are more of them latching onto me and challenging me because I'm too strong. The harder I fight, the more demons he sends to me. I cannot battle them on my own, there's too many now. Kill me now," he said.

"I will not kill you. We love you and we will not let it take you. I will fix this," I said. I kissed his lips and left out of his room after I got dressed. Elle and Amadi walked down the hall.

"He's getting weaker. This morning he almost attacked Kanya and Goon stepped in. I don't think Kanye is in there anymore," Elle said.

"He's in there, hanging on. He's still going in and out," Amadi said.

"We have two more days," I said.

"I know we are holding a meeting later with the rest of the packs around the area. We will have to come together to kill those things," he replied. After I talked to Amadi and Elle, I left and went home. When I got home, I felt like there was something out of place. I looked around and noticed a hole was in my window. I walked to it and blew on it and the glass repaired. Something flew passed my head and landed on the wall in front of me; it was a bat. The bat flew off the wall and shifted into human form and it was my mother. She stood in front of me, naked, with black eyes.

"I will find the bat cave tonight. Ula said vampires stay in dark places in the mountains where the bat caves are," she said.

"If we attack before the blood moon, it will give us a chance. The demons that are attacking Kanye will weaken and he will be able to fight them. But as long as Osiris feeds on blood, the demons will remain stronger," I said.

My body started changing. I was slimmer, with long and sandy brown hair and I was also taller in height. I was a Caucasian woman with red eyes and sharp teeth.

"How do I look?" I asked.

"Like a demon. Now we must go. I saw hundreds of bats headed to the mountains by the college you all go to. If we follow them, they could lead us to the rest of the vampires," she said. She turned into a bat and I spread my long trench coat so that she could latch on. I opened the window and floated through the air and into the woods. We followed the direction where the bats were flying up in the mountains. When we got inside the cave, there were a lot of wolf men with red eyes, feeding on humans. A few humans laid on the wet floor of the cave, tied and gagged. Osiris stood and watched with two ebony women, Yardi standing next to him.

"Keep feeding!" Osiris yelled at the wolf men.

Kanye is weak because this asshole is feeding the Underworld a human buffet, I thought.

There's too many to kill, our energy will weaken. We need to figure out how to get rid of most of them behind Osiris's back, my mother thought.

I have an idea, I replied.

Arya

The pack headed out for a meeting with the other packs that were nearby. I stayed behind because the burning desire to mate was putting a strain on me. All I wanted was the wolf that I was supposed to mate with. I tried other wolves but it didn't compare to how my body felt around Kanye. I walked out of my room and knocked on his door. Moments later, he snatched the door open. He was dressed in a hoodie, jeans, and a pair of Timbs. He had the hood pulled over his head.

"What do you want?" he asked and I opened up my black, silk robe.

"We are home alone," I said.

"You are home alone, I'm not. I'm taking my black ass back home to Monifa," he said and walked away. I grabbed his hand.

"The demon that's fighting with you wants me. Let him have me and you can have Monifa," I said. He walked away from me and I pulled him back. I grabbed his dick and it was hard. I unzipped his pants and reached inside to massage it. My body broke out in a sweat and I was burning up like I had a fever.

"You've got two seconds to get the fuck away from me or I will snap your head off. I'm trying to fight this and you are teasing it! Get the hell away from me!" he yelled.

He fell forward landing on his hands and his bones cracked while he burst out of his clothes— his body shifted. I backed away from him and his large beast stared at me with one blue eye, the other red. My heart almost stopped because his beast was too large for me to defeat. His face was in a scowl and he growled at me. I shifted and ran down the hall. His large beast chased after me and I burst through the window. I ran into the woods and he leaped up into a tree. I stopped running and looked around when his growls stopped. I heard a branch break and looked up. He jumped on me and sank his teeth into my shoulder. He slung me into a tree and the tree snapped in half. He howled at the moon before he shifted to his human form. My blood dripped from his mouth onto his chest. Both of his eyes were red and empty. I slowly turned back into human form. He grabbed me by the hair to pull me up from the ground. I tried to loosen my hair from his grip while my feet dangled above the ground.

"You little bitch," he said. His voice was deeper and it echoed throughout the woods.

"You are scaring me!" I cried and he laughed.

"After you just offered yourself to me?" he asked and dropped me.

"Stand up and face the tree," he said. I slowly stood up and turned my back towards him. He gripped my hips and licked my neck. I moaned when his strong hands squeezed my breasts. He spread me and without warning, he rammed his huge dick inside of me.

"ARRGGHHHHHHHHHHH!" I cried out when my body went limp. I immediately had an orgasm because of how bad I wanted him inside of me. He pumped in and out of me and I closed my eyes. Through closed lids, I saw a dark figure with red eyes begging me to come to him.

Give him your soul, it chanted. I opened my eyes and my body trembled from another orgasm. He grew inside of me and I gasped. I felt myself opening for him and he went further inside of me. I clawed at the tree while Kanye rammed himself in and out of me. I didn't care about anything else, just the ache I had for him. He spread my bottom and stuck two fingers inside of my anus. I screamed out and my essence dripped down my leg. My eyes rolled into the back of my head and it was the best feeling I'd ever experienced. I fell to the side and he caught me. He held me up as he continued to drill himself inside of me. My stomach cramped and I burst into tears when I had the strongest orgasm in all of my life. I fought to keep my eyes open because I didn't want to see that dark shadow with the red eyes anymore. Kanye growled and his semen filled me up. He pulled out of me and I collapsed. He looked at me with shame-filled blue eyes.

"Kanye, is that you?" I asked.

"What did I do, Arya?" he asked when he saw the blood on my shoulder.

"It's okay, it's just a small wound," I said and stood up. Kanye leaned forward and spit up blood. He gripped his stomach and fell over into the pile of leaves. I rushed to him and his body was weak. He almost went limp inside my arms.

"Get away from him," a voice said. When I turned around, it was Kanya. I stood up and tried to cover myself with my hands.

"You screwed my son anyway? After you realized he's Monifa soulmate? You held him when he was a little baby. You are too old for my son!" she yelled at me. She rushed to Kanye and took her jacket off. She covered the bottom half of him and pulled him up.

"I couldn't control it! My body craved him so much!" I cried.

"If your blood was Egyptian, you would've understood the gods and why they pick specific soulmates for us. What if you are carrying his pup? A pup with demon blood. What if you give birth to it and it has to live here? A demon pup, Arya!" she screamed.

"Take me to Monifa," Kanye said to his mother and she walked him into the house. When I turned around, Baneet stared at me with hateful eyes. I didn't realize she was with Kanya.

"Monifa is like our sister," she said.

"I'm your sister," I replied.

"I just want you to know that Monifa probably saw you screw her mate in the woods like some common whore," she screamed.

"Shut up, Baneet! I'm a whore? I know about the other wolf you have been sleeping with. He is the real reason why you don't want Zaan to mark you," I spat and she gasped.

"What I do outside of this pack is my business! I will never betray anyone the way you just did," she replied.

"You betray Zaan every chance you get!" I shouted.

"When Monifa beats your ass, I will not help you," she said and walked away.

****

Later on that night...

The rest of the pack walked into the mansion an hour later from the meeting they had with the other wolves. Goon's mother, Naobi, walked in with her mate, Kumba, and another man. I knew by the stranger's scent he was an animal but he wasn't a wolf. Naobi looked at me and I looked away. She always crept me out because when she looked at someone, she was looking into their soul. Elle and Amadi served everyone drinks and raw meat on a tray. They were still discussing their attack on the vampires. I got up to use the bathroom. After I was finished, I washed my hands then headed to my room. When I walked inside, Naobi was sitting on my bed, staring at me.

"Hey, how can I help you?" I asked.

"This isn't a drive-thru restaurant, so you can drop the greeting. Sit down next to me, Chile, so we can talk," she said.

"I can stand," I replied.

"I guess you really enjoyed my grandson's beast if you can't sit down," she said and stood up. She walked around my room with her long gold and blue gown dragging the floor behind her.

"What are you doing in my room?" I asked and she laughed.

"When you were a little girl, I always knew you would be trouble. Your heart isn't dark and neither is it pure. It's not your fault, I remember what Sosa did to you. He taught you how to use your body at a young age, and even after all the love the pack showed you, that part of you is still curious. He brainwashed you," she said.

"I hated Sosa, so don't you ever bring him up to me again," I said and wiped my eyes.

"I'm going to bring him up because what he did is the cause of your actions. I can't see your visions because your blood isn't from my gods and I'm not connected to you spiritually, but I don't have to be because your actions speak for you," she said.

"What actions are you talking about because what I did was based off tradition. I don't know anything about Egyptian gods because my tribe were Indians," I said.

"Even a human with no religion knows that if a man's heart belongs to another then it belongs to another. You can offer yourself to him but he will still feel a spiritual bond with the one he loves. This is not about tradition; this is about being a pure woman. I'm trying to save your soul before the demon that you slept with tonight poisons it. Demons love females like you. They'll trap you in their world and rape you every second until you have nothing! It will make your heart so black that there won't be no coming back. Sosa will be like a god compared to those demons. The ones that possessed Kanye felt the inside of you tonight. They felt your spirit and they know you can be sold by lust," she said. She opened my hand and dropped a necklace into it.

"This is 'Sa', the symbol for protection. Hopefully, it can protect you," she said and walked to my door.

"I thought we couldn't be protected from demons," I said and she turned around.

"This is protection from yourself. You are your own demon, Arya. I have to get going now. My grandson needs me," she said and walked out.

****

The next morning, I went hunting in the woods. I crept behind a deer and a tiger leaped out the bushes and attacked it. The tiger's big paws crushed the deer's neck then it tore into it. I went behind the bushes where my clothes were and got dressed.

"Kumba, I wanted that," I said when I stepped out of the bushes. The tiger's green eyes looked at me and stepped away from the deer. The tiger went behind a tree and when he came back in man form, he was dressed in pants and it wasn't Kumba.

"I'm sorry about that. Do you forgive me? My name is Taj. I'm Kumba's cousin. I introduced myself to everyone last night but you disappeared," he said. Taj was tall, extremely tall. He stood at six-foot-six and was the color of sand. His hair was in locks and they came down passed his shoulders. His eyes were emerald green. He had tiger-stripe markings all over his body. He was almost as beautiful as Kanye.

"I'm Arya and nice to meet you," I said and walked off. He followed behind me.

"I left you some," he said and chuckled.

"I don't eat after strangers," I replied.

"In animal kingdom, it's all about surviving," he said and I giggled.

"How old are you, Taj?" I asked. If he was a human, I would've thought early twenties but a thousand-year-old immortal still looked young.

"I'm one hundred years old. I'm the youngest out of my cousins," he said.

"Not bad," I replied.

"And you are a pup?" he asked.

"I'm thirty years old, literally," I said.

"You are a pup," he said and I rolled my eyes.

"What brings you here?" I asked.

"I moved into the city a few weeks ago to help Kumba with his restaurant chain. I wanted to meet the pack sooner but I had a lot of unfinished business back home," he said.

"Your mate?" I asked and he chuckled.

"Is that your way of finding out if I'm single," he said.

"Don't flatter yourself. You are a hundred years old, I'm sure you have a family of your own," I said.

"Nope, no family," he said and he stared at me.

"You have beautiful eyes," he flirted and I looked away.

"Thank you," I said and walked off. I wasn't used to a man giving me compliments other than how great my body was. Taj followed me into the house. I grabbed a pitcher of water out of the fridge and he sat down at the kitchen island. I was getting agitated by him.

"Why are you watching me?" I asked.

"Cats like watching when there's something that catches the eye. So, tell me more about you, Miss Arya. Are you mated with anyone? Do you have any pups?" he asked.

"I'm single and I'm in heat. There, you have it, now is there anything else you want to know?" I asked.

"Nope, have a good day," he said and walked out of the kitchen. Chancy came into the kitchen and sat down at the island.

"I don't like cats but Taj is very handsome," she said.

"He's aight," I said.

"What's going on with you? I heard what happened last night. Father is very pissed off at you and even thought about coming into your room with a belt last night, but Goon told him that the pack had other shit to worry about," she said.

"I don't regret giving myself to Kanye. I can't help how I feel about him. Do you know how it feels to want something so bad that you will do anything to get it? That's how I feel. I will not turn those feelings off. Why is no one taking my feelings into consideration? Everything is about Monifa and the gods. Fuck their gods and all of that other ancient ancestor shit! What good has it done for them anyway? Anubi is supposed to be like heaven and it sounds to me like it's all a hoax. This pack is brainwashing us," I said.

"Our father is a part of Anubi, Arya. Don't speak on the gods that way. Their plan was for Monifa and Kanye. Why do you think she feels what he feels? Why do you think she has the same markings as him? If it's not the gods doing, then what is it?" Chancy asked.

"It's their damn magic that's doing it. I believe they cast these spells and do what they want then blame it on the gods. Kanye and Monifa hated each other and now he loves her and wants to give her pups? That is bullshit!" I said.

"She does have a point," Ula said when she walked into the kitchen. Her heels clicked across the floor and her hair was straightened down her back. She reminded me of a video vixen in a rap video.

"Thank you," I said and she smiled.

"I'm not agreeing with you, honey, you just have a point. Make yourself believe what you want to believe but love doesn't lie. Looking for reasons to justify sleeping with someone's soulmate is doing nothing but brainwashing yourself. You want to believe the gods don't exist, but they do; trust me, I know. I don't agree with Anubi but that doesn't mean what they stand for is a hoax," Ula said.

"You are a witch. I've learned not to trust witches," I said.

"And I've learned to not give two fucks about anybody's opinion but Amadi's," she said.

"I guess you think I've forgotten how you haunted him when he was with Jesula. You call that love?" I asked and Chancy shook her head.

"Yes, I call that love and here is why. I could've killed him, I could've killed Jesula, and I could've done everything else to destroy him but I didn't because I loved him. I wanted him to see that I was still holding on to him but not once did I think about cursing him. I only haunted him because he allowed me to. He couldn't let me go, either. So, what do you call that?" Ula asked.

"Witchcraft," I said and her eyes turned pitch-black. A snake appeared around her neck and the glass pitcher shattered on the table. Ten snakes slithered up my body and I screamed. Seconds later, they disappeared and she laughed at me.

"That's witchcraft and I would love to stay and show you more but I have to talk with my sister, Naobi," she said and disappeared.

"Damn, I don't like witches," I said.

"I don't think you like anyone. What happened to you? Why are you speaking badly about the people that you lived with for twenty years? Ula might be a bit sarcastic all of the time but she's always there if you need her. What she did to Amadi turned out for the better. You see how happy he is with her," Chancy said.

"Get out of my face, Chancy. I want to be alone," I said and she walked out of the kitchen. I grabbed my shoes, purse, and car keys and headed out of the door to Laura's house.

****

"So, the pack is trying to figure out a way to take down the vampires?" Laura asked while I laid on her couch, venting.

"Yes," I replied.

"What a shame. Where is Kanye at now?" Laura asked.

"At his home, the one he shares with Monifa," I said.

"So, you slept with him and might be carrying his pup?" she asked.

"My body doesn't feel the craving anymore, so maybe I am. I don't know, but I do know that I'm tired of all this tradition bullshit," I spat. She sat down next to me and handed me a glass of wine.

"Go out on your own, that way Kanye can come to you whenever he wants to. If the demon is still in him, he will have you again. They crave sex," she said.

"How do you know?" I asked.

"I read a lot of books. All you have to do is give yourself to him. Offer your soul and he will forget all about Monifa. Demons love sacrifices and will cherish you forever because of it," she said. I pulled out the necklace Naobi gave to me from underneath my shirt. It probably was a curse because witches were conniving. I showed it to Laura.

"Naobi gave this to me. She said it will protect me," I said. Laura looked at the necklace and smiled.

"She did that to brainwash you," she said.

"I don't know what to do," I said.

"We will figure it out but in the meantime, let's go to a party," she said. She went into her room and came back with a red dress. She held it up in front of her.

"What do you think?" she asked.

"It's okay, red is not really my color," I said.

"Oh, girl, I love red," she said and I yawned. All of a sudden, I was very tired and I couldn't keep my eyes open. I fell asleep on Laura's couch.

****

I woke up and looked around. My head was spinning and it felt like a heavy brick was on my legs. I tried to move but I couldn't. The room was dark and the sounds of chains clanked when I moved my arms. I tried to shift but I couldn't; something was keeping me from shifting. I screamed for help.

"HELP!" The light came on and I was inside of a room chained to a bed. Candles were lined up around the room and fresh roses covered my naked body. I burst into tears and screamed louder for help.

"It's okay, dear," the voice said.

"What are you doing to me, Laura?" I asked. She floated toward me and stood next to the bed, wearing a black, hooded cape. She pulled the hood back and she turned into an ebony woman with long, white locks and black eyes. She smiled at me and a book appeared in her hands. The book was made out of leather and had hieroglyphics on the front of it.

"Laura is dead. I used her body to get closer to you," she said. She sat a medium-sized glass ball on my chest.

"I want you to watch everything inside of this globe," she said. I looked at the globe and I saw images of wolf men. I also saw myself in a lab helping to create them.

"I don't remember that!" I yelled at her.

"I know. I took the memory away from you so that you wouldn't crack and tell your pack everything about the wolf men. I also didn't want you to remember seeing me that night in the lab. I had to protect my identity," she said.

"What is your name?" I asked.

"Meda. I am Ammon's daughter and all I want is enough of Goon's blood to reincarnate Ammon. Goon's blood is the key. I would've used Baki's but he isn't capable enough to bring back an immortal like Ammon. The spell wouldn't work, but with Goon's, it will," she said. She brushed the roses off my stomach and my eyes almost bulged out of my head. My stomach was the size of a soccer ball.

"What is this?" I cried.

"No need to cry. You wanted a pup by Kanye and now you got it. Immortal babies grow fast, especially demon pups. You will give birth soon," she said.

"Why do you have me here? I thought we were friends! I told you everything!" I yelled at her and she laughed.

"I actually like you, Arya. We are almost the same. I feel out of place in Anubi the same way you feel out of place with your pack. I think we should work together," she said. I hulked up a glob of spit and spat in her face. It dripped down her cheek and onto her lip. She made it disappear and I felt a force choking me.

"I should kill you! I'm trying to save your life! Do you think I want to do this? No, I don't, but I have to!" she screamed and the bed shook. The force stopped choking me and I started coughing.

"You don't have to do this," I said.

"Seth is making me do it! You just don't get it. I have an evil warlock spirit latched on to me and he made a deal with Seth many ages ago. He told Seth that he would help him be free from the Underworld if he gave him the ability to practice black magic. Seth granted Musaf his wish but Musaf reincarnated himself into me, making me Seth's property. What Seth wants, I have to give to him. Seth wants Ammon to be born again but as a demon. Ammon will be a great warrior for the Underworld. An ancient beast in the Underworld is like hitting the jackpot of demons. He can't use Goon because Goon's heart is too pure. Ammon's heart was blacker than coal," she said.

"If it's not your doing, why do you hate Goon so much?" I asked.

"Because he should've killed me! I hate everyone in Anubi! They knew what was inside of me and wanted me to live to feel the pain and torture! You want to know how it feels to be a baby and see images of demons in your sleep? Do you know how it feels to have Seth own your body against your will? When I was sixteen, my soul was trapped inside a dungeon for five days, and in those five days, those things did whatever they wanted to me. I was born a slave to a demon," she said. She pulled out the necklace Naobi gave to me out of her pocket.

"Where was my protection from them?" she cried. Black tears slipped from her eyes.

"This is not you, Meda. We can help you," I said and she laughed.

"Help me? Nobody can help me, Arya. Nobody cared to help me. I accepted my role in all of this and Seth gets whatever Seth wants," she said and the room went dark again. I screamed at the top of my lungs but something covered my mouth.

I'm sorry, Arya, Meda thought. I felt small flutters inside of me coming from my pup. I had to save my pup from the Underworld.

Akea

We had a day and a half left until the blood moon rose. The pack was preparing themselves for war against the vampire-wolf hybrids.

"Are you sure you will be safe with Kanye?" my father asked me.

"Yes, Father, I will be fine," I said and he placed his hand on my shoulder.

"I know you will, you are a strong boy. You don't see it but I do. We will kill as many vampires as we can to weaken that thing that's latched on to your brother then we will go from there. I don't want you to leave, I want you to stay here with Chancy, Baneet, and Zaan. This battle is not for you all," he said.

"Okay, Father," I said and he left Monifa and Kanye's apartment. I shut the door and Zaan, Chancy, and Baneet stared at me.

"This sucks!" Chancy said.

"Tell me about it. We are practically grown and still have to sit back like fucking pups," Zaan fussed and rolled up a blunt. Kanye sat at the kitchen table, drinking a glass of Hennessey. He looked defeated. I sat down next to him and he slid the bottle to me.

"They are only defeating you because of all the blood the wolf men have taken from the humans. The bloodshed is giving the Underworld strength. Once the hybrids are dead, you will be okay," I said.

"They left me alone for now. Monifa is blocked from my thoughts and I'm blocked from hers," he stressed.

"We don't have connections to that side of the world. Once a demon interferes with your life, your thoughts belong to them and so does your visions," I said.

"She can feel me, though, bro. I can't believe I fucked Arya. That was the worse shit I could ever do while having this thing inside of me. That bitch knew it wanted her and she acted on it," he spat and took another sip of his liquor. His eyes turned red and his teeth sharpened. He flipped the table over and glass shattered onto the floor. He picked up the chairs and hurled them into the walls. One chair went through the window and landed on a car in the parking lot, triggering the car alarm. Kanye's temper was getting out of control. Zaan growled at him.

"Calm down, Zaan," I said.

"That's not Kanye, bro," Zaan said.

"Are you challenging me, muthafucka?" Kanye asked. Baneet ran off into the corner and Chancy stood in the middle of the floor next to Zaan.

"Kanye, I know you are in there but I'm warning you! If this thing that's inside of you fucks with any of us, I will fight you," Chancy said and Kanye laughed.

"Get your bitch, Akea," Kanye said.

"This is scaring me!" Baneet cried.

"Shut the fuck up, whore. Do you want to know the real reason why Kanye feels like you are trash? It's because he caught you fucking another wolf in the woods while he was hunting," Kanye said.

"WHAT!" Zaan shouted.

"It's trying to turn us against each other, Zaan. That is not Kanye speaking, it's the demon," I said to him. Zaan looked at Baneet and his eyes glowed when his teeth sharpened.

"Is this true, Baneet?" Zaan asked and she looked away from him.

"Is it true, damn it!" Zaan yelled at her and she jumped.

"I'm sorry, Zaan, but it's complicated. I'm not ready for all of this," Baneet said.

"Don't believe that whore, Zaan. She just thinks the other wolf fucks her better," Kanye said and laughed.

Baneet charged into Kanye and he caught her by the throat. He choke-slammed her into a wall and she fell through it. Chancy jumped on him and scratched his face and he flung her into the kitchen like a rag doll. I sent an electrical bolt into his chest but he didn't fall.

"Really, nigga? It's just pussy, and speaking of pussy. I think I should go and find Arya. She knows how to give herself away," he said.

"Where is Kanye?" I asked.

"Fighting for his life again. But I think this time, he won't make it," it said.

"Do something, Akea!" Chancy cried when she helped her sister out of the wall.

"I don't know what to do!" I yelled at her. Ula told me to get inside of Kanye but I didn't know how to. Naobi told me to connect my energy with his, but I couldn't. I was my brother's only hope and I couldn't save him.

Kanye's eyes turned blue again and he fell to the floor. I ran over to him and lifted his head up.

"Wake up!" I said to him but his pulse was weakening.

"Do something, Akea!" Zaan pleaded.

"I don't know what to do!" I yelled.

"Figure it out! I don't think he is going to make it!" Zaan fussed.

You two are connected. You are a part of his beast and he is a part of you. I remembered what Ula said to me.

"Give me a knife," I shouted out.

"For what?" Chancy asked.

"It doesn't matter, just give me one!" I yelled at her. She went into the kitchen drawer and grabbed me a knife. She handed it to me and I cut my wrist as deep as I could go. I lifted Kanye's head up and put my wrist to his mouth.

"Drink my blood, Kanye. Drink as much as you can," I said.

"That doesn't work!" Baneet spat.

"He didn't drink enough the first time. My energy source is in my blood. I'm his other half and if I give him my energy, it attracts his energy like a magnet and those things will not be able to possess him anymore. They cannot defeat a greater force. Me and Kanye together is the same as our father's strength," I replied.

"I don't want to, just set me on fire. I don't want you to be a part of this," Kanye said weakly.

"Drink enough until you feel my energy," I said and Chancy looked at me.

"Are you sacrificing yourself?" she asked me.

"No, I'm joining him to defeat the visions he has of those demons," I said. I placed my arm to Kanye's mouth.

"Think about Monifa," I said and he sank his canines into my wrist. He drank until I felt what was a part of him. Through his vision, I saw him inside of a dark, small cage and he was exhausted. The black shadows with the red eyes kept going in and out of his body, trying to steal his soul. They could enter his body but they couldn't stay because he was still fighting them. He looked weak to us but he wasn't weak enough for the demons. Kanye's beast was too stubborn to let them take him. Vampires could only latch on to the weak. If your soul was resistant, they would try to break you down until there wasn't any strength left. They were getting angry with Kanye because his strength wasn't fading away so easily.

Give it up, Kanye! You can't reject us for too long, the voice said to him.

Fuck you, punk! I'm not giving up, so we can do this all fucking night! Kanye replied and the voice laughed at him.

You are getting weak, it said.

But I'm not giving up, Kanye replied.

Let him go! I said.

I will once he gives me his body, it responded.

Get out of here, Akea! Kanye said.

What is this place? I asked.

Welcome to hell, the voice replied.

You can't keep him here, his heart is pure and that's why your demons can't stay inside of him, I replied.

Allow your energy to connect to mine. Don't reject it, just let it happen! I said to Kanye.

The dark shadows tried to enter Kanye's body again but they couldn't go through him. Our energy was pulling together and forming a knot. My body started to feel light as Kanye continued to drink my blood. I saw visions of me being a beast and it was the same beast as Kanye's. I disappeared inside of him...

Kanye

I gasped for air when I sat up off the floor. I looked around the place and I was still at home. I felt my face and my arms, because my body didn't feel the same. Zaan, Baneet, and Chancy stared at me with confusion. I slowly stood up and they continued to stare at me without blinking.

"I feel different," I said.

"Akea disappeared," Zaan said.

"Where did he go?" I asked.

"He's inside of you," Chancy said in disbelief.

Bro, this is some real freaky sci-fi shit! And it is freaking cool! Bro, remember the Power Rangers *and how the rangers morphed and got inside of their dinosaurs? Well, bro, I just got inside of you. I know what my dream meant now, I'm a part of you. We are a part of each other,"* Akea's voice said inside of my head.

"What the hell! Oh, hell nawl! Y'all get this nigga out of me!" I said and Akea laughed.

Is that the thanks I get after helping your soul leave the Underworld? Our blood together is like father's, he said. I held my hands out and electricity formed at the tips of my fingers. Baneet fainted.

Okay, now you can come out, I said to Akea.

I'm stuck. I got inside of you but I don't know how to get out, he said.

Y'all niggas just like my body, don't y'all? At first it was those black shadows with red eyes, and now I'm possessed by my brother?" I asked.

Ummm, I guess so, but I will figure it out. Let me think—oh and your eyesight is way better than mine. Tell Chancy she looks super sexy in that outfit, he said.

"Akea said you look sexy as fuck in that outfit," I said to Chancy.

Bro, I didn't say that! Akea yelled.

I know but you need to put some "umph" into your swag. That's why she bosses you around. I'm telling you, bro, females like dominant males, I replied.

"This is a freaking nightmare! Akea, please come out!" Chancy yelled into my ear.

"He is trying to figure it out," I said. I swiped my hand across the room and all of the broken items went back together like nothing ever happened.

You can control me, too? I asked.

This is super sweet! he replied.

"My life is ruined. I'm being haunted by a damn geek," I said and helped Baneet off the floor.

What are you doing? Leave her ass there, I thought.

We can't leave her like this, Akea replied.

"Welcome back, bro!" Zaan finally said and Chancy rolled her eyes.

"I'm very happy you are back and feeling better, but I would like my boyfriend back now. Tell Akea he had his little fun but now he needs to get out of you," Chancy said.

"I want him out just as much as you do. He is too excited," I replied. I opened the window and looked toward the mountains where the bat caves were. It was night time and I howled at the moon.

Stop that shit! I still have to live in this building, I thought.

I always wanted to do that, Akea replied.

Wait until I get in the woods, idiot! I replied but I was thankful for him.

Ummm, I'm waiting for you to shift, he said growing impatient. My bones snapped and I burst out of my clothes, I crouched down and my face turned into a snout. My nails sharpened and my hair pierced through my skin like needles. I shook the shredded clothes off of myself and my beast leaped out of the window.

Slow down! he complained.

You wanted to be a beast, so you better enjoy it, bro, I said and kept running. Zaan, Chancy, and Baneet ran behind me in beast form. We leaped up into the trees and ran until we were a few miles away from the bat caves. I heard growling from behind me and it was Daja and her pack brothers. One of her brother's beasts growled at me and a bolt of blue lightning came from my eyes. The other wolves stepped back and growled at us.

We are here to defeat the wolf men, her brother finally said. About thirty more wolves came from behind the trees in the woods. All of our packs were combined. I heard a deep, hoarse howl and I knew who it was; it was my father with his pack. The bats flew from the trees and the moon hid behind the clouds. It was a chilly night and fog came out of our snouts as we breathed in the night air. My father and his pack brothers were the biggest beasts in the woods. His black beast blended in with the night and his blue eyes glowed.

Akea cured me, I said.

I felt it the moment he did. I knew he was going to figure it out. You two joined are a greater force, he said.

How does he get out of me? I asked.

The question is, does he really want to? My father chuckled. His beast walked passed me and climbed onto a rock. His tall beast sat up and looked around at all of the beasts in the crowd.

Glad we can all come together. Tonight is not about who the greater alpha is; it's about protecting our families—our packs. We don't have to like each other tomorrow but tonight we are family! Those hybrids are the enemies and we will kill as many as we can, and will not stop until they are dead, he said and all the wolves howled. Kumba and his cousin, Taj, walked through the crowd of wolves and a few wolves growled at them.

They are family! my father said. Baneet and Chancy were ordered to go home but they didn't leave. They wanted to stay and fight, too. Zaan told his father that he was fighting and Elle left him alone.

Welcome back, Monifa's voice said.

Where are you, I need to see you, I said.

Behind you, she said. When I turned around, a white woman with long, brown hair and red eyes stared at me from behind a bush.

Monifa? I asked. I walked over to her and she kneeled down in front of me. Her eyes turned back to their normal color.

Are you a vampire? I asked.

No, she's able to disguise herself as one, Akea said.

Mind your business, I spat. Monifa wrapped her arms around my beast's neck and squeezed me.

Me and my mother had been in the caves and around the woods. There are so many of those wolf men, plus two witches with Osiris from Anubi. It's going to be hard to defeat them but I think we can all lure them into the caves and then block them in after we set them all on fire and send them back to hell, she said.

That's going to take a lot of force, Akea thought.

"Wait, I heard Akea's voice in your thoughts. Where is he?" she asked.

Inside of me. It's hard to explain but we are combined and he is liking it a bit too much, I replied and she laughed.

"I bet he is. You don't know how much I've missed you. It was only a few days but those few days felt like forever. I wasn't able to hear your thoughts and I felt like a part of me was trapped, too," she said. I dropped my head down in shame. I rubbed my head against her arm and my wolf whined like he was wounded.

I did a terrible thing and I don't think you will ever forgive me. I don't think I will ever forgive myself because of what the outcome will be, I thought and she stepped back from me.

Bro, are you ready to tell her this now? Akea asked.

I don't know what we will happen after this night and I need to tell her before she finds out on her own. I can't keep nothing away from her. I love her, I replied.

"What happened?" Monifa asked with tears falling down her face. Deep down I knew she knew and I hated that I had to tell her, but it was my only way. I didn't want the burden hanging over my head.

Arya and I mated and she's carrying my pup. As soon as Akea healed me, I saw a vision of our pup inside of her womb, I replied. Monifa fell down into the grass on her knees and her hair blew. She turned back into herself and her long locks fell down, covering her face.

"It hurts!" she screamed and the tree next to her broke in half. Lightning from the sky struck the ground in front of me. Her eyes and tears turned black.

"My heart is broken. I have been out here trying to find an answer to all of this. My identity could've been figured out when I was inside of that cave but not once did I care. All I wanted was for you to be cured and for those things to burn so they could never come back to us again. Love is the greatest evil. It hurts more than anything! It burns your soul when someone betrays your heart. It weakens your mind and it makes your heart turn black. The demons cannot do anything like that, but what the gods praise the most can. I wish you the best of luck. After this fight, you will never see me again. I know it wasn't your fault but if we were destined to be, it wouldn't have happened. Maybe our meaning of each other was a mistake," she said and disappeared.

I'm sorry, bro, but she's just mad. Monifa will not let you go that easily, Akea thought.

I felt every word she said to me. I felt every ounce of hate she had inside of her. Monifa doesn't want me anymore. You think I wanted to burn because of the demon? I wanted to burn because I knew the demon wanted Arya. It saw how easily she was willing to give herself to it. I knew I was going to end up hurting Monifa. I'd rather go back to hell before I watch her move on. I love her more than she loves me, I thought. A tear fell from my beast's eyes and landed on my paw. Beast never cries! In human form we felt emotions but our beast was emotionless.

That bond is strong, bro, anytime your beast weeps. That's a sign from the gods, Kanye. They are showing you that you cannot give up on her because you two are destined to be together. Fight for her, Akea thought.

Monifa

"Where are you going?" my mother asked me. She shifted from her bat and into her human form. I was walking through the woods in what seemed like a circle.

"I'm going far away to connect with myself," I said.

"That's what Keora did when she realized the man she loved had a soulmate. She tried to deal with heartbreak alone and ended up practicing black magic. I see more and more of her inside of you now. Don't go down the same path she went down. Your heart is pure and you are so innocent," my mother said and I wiped my tears away.

"Maybe that path will make me numb, Mother. I went through every experience with Kanye. He deflowered me, he made love to my body, mind, and soul. We had a connection and I got his markings. Those markings hurt more than anyone can imagine. My skin felt like it was on fire. I've been losing my mind over him and look what I get? Nothing but emptiness. Maybe Keora did the right thing when she went away," I spat.

"No, she didn't," a voice said from behind me. When I turned around, it was Naobi. I bowed my head to her and she walked over to me.

"No need for that, Chile. I'm not higher than you," she said. She held my chin up with the tip of her nail and she stared deeply into my eyes.

"What we fail to realize as immortals is that shit happens. We think because we are immortals everything should be easy. The gods give us a soulmate and just like that, we expect things to be perfect. That was Keora's problem. She thought because we were immortals we were in higher power. We feel what anyone with a heart feels. We get depressed, we cry, we get mad, and we feel alone. The beauty of our love is that it lasts for eternity; that's the only difference between us and the humans. The gods show us who our perfect match is and after that, their job is done. Keora didn't understand that she had to wait for her time to come and she let her magic control her. She made herself believe that she could force it. You can't force something that's not meant to be, just like it's not meant for you to be without Kanye. You can go away and be alone, but you will still yearn for him. Your souls are connected, and once that happens, only death can break you two apart. Now, hold your head up high and straighten your shoulders," she said and I stood up straighter.

"It will be a cold day in hell if I give up on you like I did Keora. Seeing you is like seeing her, and I loved her with everything I had in me. Even after everything she did, I still loved her. I will not let her soul make the same mistake it made before," she said.

"I understand," I said.

"Good, well understand that the pup inside of Arya is not really Kanye's. It might look like him when it's born but it belongs to the demon that invaded his body when he mated with her. That demon is going to want his pup. His pup belongs to the Underworld and Arya belongs to the thing that she gave her body to," Naobi said and my mother grabbed her chest.

"This is too much," my mother said.

"The pack was looking for her before they came here. Something tells me Arya is in trouble," Naobi said. The sounds of growling and the smell of blood filled the air.

"The fight has begun. You two be careful and I will look for Arya," Naobi said and disappeared. My mother turned into a large Egyptian Mau and I turned into my beast. It was time to battle. We ran through the woods, toward the mountains with the bat caves. Growling and howling echoed throughout the mountains. We rushed into the cave and it was horrific. Blood was everywhere and the smell of open flesh filled my nostrils. Wolf men were biting the wolves and the wolves were shredding them to pieces. One of the witches with Osiris tried to use her magic on a wolf but I shielded it. The witch looked at me with black eyes and she sent a bolt of lightning toward me but a shield covered me. I ran up the wall inside the cave and leaped onto her. I sank my teeth into her throat and a wolf man swatted my face; I felt my flesh tearing apart. Blood dripped down my face and splashed onto my paws. Kanye's beast leaped over the brawl and tackled the wolf man that injured me. His beast ripped the wolf man in half. The witch crawled away from me but I jumped on her back and bit the back of her neck. A force threw me across the cave and my beast landed inside a puddle of muddy water. The witch appeared in front of me and a bolt of lightning appeared in her hand. She swung it at me and I howled as it burned my flesh.

I turned back into human form, wearing a hooded brown cape.

"I'm going to send your ass back to Anubi, bitch!" I said and I charged into her. I slammed her face into the stone wall and dark-red blood squirted from her nose. My nails sharpened and I grabbed her by the throat. I felt a bolt enter me through my back and it exited out of my chest. I fell onto the ground and the witch stood over me. A beautiful ebony witch with white locks appeared over me and stood next to the witch I attacked.

"Kill her Jutu and do it now," the witch said. Jutu looked at me and I looked into her eyes.

"You were once pure. I can see it in your eyes that this is not you. Anubi is your home and these things are going to destroy it if you don't help us," I pleaded with Jutu. The witch with the white locks pulled out a dagger with red jewels embedded inside the handle. She kneeled down next to me. She dragged her knife down my face.

"The famous Monifa. The one that Arya despise so much. You should see how pretty she looks with a swollen belly. Kanye really couldn't resist her. He wanted her more than he wanted you. What a pity," she said and she turned into Arya's friend Laura.

"I've been around longer than you know. My name is Meda but you can call me Laura," she said and turned back into herself. Arya was friends with a traitor.

"You know I looked up to you, well, Keora. I heard great stories about her black magic. She was almost my hero until Naobi brainwashed her; tricked her into becoming this weak, little witch. How do you lose someone who was made for you and marked by the gods for you? Keora would've never settled for that. Why don't you join us? I know you feel lonely now that your mate mated with someone else," she said.

"You have lost your mind," I spat.

"Black magic is not that bad. It takes away the pain. It makes you not feel anything. I can sense you are tempted," she said.

"Get your wicked ass away from me, bitch!" I yelled at her and her body slammed into the stone wall. Jutu tried to strike me with lightning but I blocked it. I sent it into her chest and she collapsed on the ground.

"After I kick your ass, I'm going to kick that bitch Arya's ass," I spat. I charged into Meda and she stabbed me with her dagger. After she pulled it out of me, my wound closed.

"Is that the best you got?" I asked and she sent a force into my chest that knocked air out of me. I felt paralyzed and blood spilled out of my mouth. Kanye's beast was being attacked by over six wolf men and the pack was fighting the rest of the wolf men off each other. Chancy and Zaan were ripping a wolf man apart. Baneet had a wolf man's arm dangling from her mouth. The wolf men kept coming and we were outnumbered. Meda held her dagger over me and she was ready to stab me in the throat. Kanye's beast charged into her and knocked her down. He clamped down on her neck and slung her into the wall. His beast was covered in blood but he still had all of his strength. Some of the blood belonged to him and some of it didn't. The bolt Meda sent into my chest felt like a heavy brick was sitting on my heart. Jutu shielded Meda from Kanye's beast and they both disappeared. Kanye shifted into his human form and carried me inside an opening in the stone wall of the cave.

He laid me down and cradled me.

"Go and help the pack," I whispered.

"Most of the wolf men are dead. We are winning," he said.

"I'm fine right here," I said.

"I can't leave you," he replied and hugged me. A tiger walked over to us and turned into a man, a man that I hadn't seen before. His locks fell down his shoulders and he stared at us with green eyes. He kneeled down next to us.

"She doesn't look too good," he said.

"Meda poisoned her to slow down her energy," Kanye replied.

"Those things are dead. A few werewolves are injured and some died, but it's over. We have to get out so your father can destroy the caves," he said. Kanye picked me up and carried me. Whatever Meda gave me was starting to burn the inside of my body. Osiris appeared in front of us with red eyes.

"The war is not over, it has just begun," he said. More wolf men came inside the cave, eyes glowing. The werewolves were tired from battling and they had to fight thirty more wolf men.

"Punk muthafucka!" Kanye said and Osiris laughed. Kanye sat me down against the bloody stone wall before he charged into Osiris. He body slammed Osiris onto the floor of the cave and it cracked. Kanye picked Osiris up by his neck then punched him in the face and he flew into the air, turning into a bat. He flew through a small crack in the cave. Two wolf men tried to attack Kanye but the tiger shifter shifted and his large body flew into the wolf men. I heard growling coming from the side of me and it was Yardi. Yardi turned into a wolf man and his red eyes glowed. His big hand picked me up by my hair and he held me up in the air like I weighed nothing. Kanye's blue eyes glowed and his canines sharpened; he was in mid-shift.

"I'm going to fight you just like this, bitch," Kanye spat. His naked body was covered in blood and a small stream of blood flowed in the lines of his six-pack stomach. Yardi tossed me down on the ground. Him and Kanye ran into each other, growling, and when they collided, it sounded like a pile of bricks slapping into each other. Kanye slammed Yardi into the wall and sent sharp jabs into his stomach. Yardi swatted at Kanye's face and put four deep slashes on his cheek. Kanye head-butted Yardi then punched him in the throat. Yardi fell down on the ground and whined. Kanye circled around him, growling.

"Get up, bitch! I knew I was going to kill you. I could taste it," Kanye spat then kicked Yardi in his deformed snout. Yardi slowly got up and swatted at Kanye. Kanye sent a hard blow into Yardi's chest and I heard something crack. Yardi fell onto the ground and he was barely alive.

Four wolf men attacked Kanye and my father's oversized beast ripped one of the men apart. Amadi and Dayo's beasts joined the brawl. Blood flew onto my face as I watched the pack rip the wolf men into shreds. Chancy's beast picked me up by the hood on my cape and tossed me over its shoulder. Kanye shifted back into his wolf form to join the pack on their killing spree.

Chancy, I think I'm going to die, I thought.

I will get you out of here. Hold tight, she thought.

Kanye

I'm losing my energy, Akea thought.

Hold tight, bro, we are ready to get out. Father is trying to get the wolves out before he destroys the cave, I replied.

Look to your right, bro. Who is that? Akea asked me. I snapped a wolf man's neck then tossed him inside of the muddy blood. I turned around and saw a woman. When she saw me, she ran. I took off after her and chased her into a dead end at the end of the cave. She fell down on the ground and bowed her head.

"You are Queen Naobi's grandson. I come in peace," she said.

Awkward, Akea thought.

Who are you? I asked her.

I'm Fiti and I'm from Anubi. Meda sent me here but my heart doesn't have the desire for all of this death. Please, just let me go, she thought and I growled.

Why should I trust you? I replied.

I know how I can get back to Anubi. I just need Naobi's help. Meda has cast a spell on everyone back home and they are in a deep sleep. I will help you if you help me return, she thought. She held out her arm then sliced it with a gold dagger. Her blood dripped onto the stone ground.

My blood is not dark like hers or Jutu's. My blood is still pure. I don't know how since she created me from her black magic spell book. But my heart doesn't desire death. I just want to go back home, she pleaded. Zaan's beast came from behind me and he walked over to Fiti. She backed away from him and she covered her face. Her body trembled and soft cries escaped her lips. Zaan's beast lifted her chin up with its snout and he licked her face.

What is Zaan doing? We are in a battle and his beast is thinking about pleasure, Akea thought.

His beast is telling her to not be afraid. He is letting her know that we will not hurt her, I thought. Fiti climbed on top of Zaan's beast's back and she pulled the hood on her cape over her head. The pack was defeating what was left of the wolf men. A wolf man slashed my father's beast across the face and I leaped onto him, burying my teeth in the back of its neck. My father's beast tore the wolf man's leg from his hip, clean off. I felt something bite my leg and it was a bat. I crushed its small skull inside of my mouth and it burst like a grape.

I'm going to be sick! That was gross! Oh, god I can taste it and it's awful, Akea thought. Another bat flew onto me and my teeth shredded it into pieces.

Where are these things coming from? I asked myself. Loud, squeaking noises filled the cave and a huge gang of bats flew into the caves, colliding with our bodies. A few of them flew into the walls and broke their necks but the rest of them were sinking their small, sharp teeth into our flesh. Fiti burned a few of them with fire that came from the palms of her hands. A wolf man tried to attack Zaan but Fiti shielded him.

Lead the wolves out of the cave and I will take it from here, my father thought.

I'm not leaving you, Father, I replied.

Now is not the time to debate with me, Kanye! Get the fuck out of the cave and do it now! his voice boomed inside of my head.

Okay, Father, but if you don't come out, I will come back for you, I said. I howled and alerted the others that the fight was over and we needed to leave. There were a few wolf men that were still alive but I trusted my father to destroy them all. I dragged Daja's brother, Geo, by the neck and out of the cave because he was injured. I knew Monifa was safe with Chancy. My mother was home at the mansion with Anik, Ula and Fabia waiting for us to return. I knew our fathers were going to get a lot of hell because we fought beside them but we were not backing down. We were no longer pups and their war was our war. We stuck together.

Osiris

I flew around the dark cave and watched the battle beneath me. The wolf men were defeated by Goon's pack. The bats attacked the wolves and a few bats turned to ashes.

We are losing! I said to Meda but she didn't answer me. I lost myself behind Meda's hatred for her brother, Goon, and his pack. I no longer cared about my beast or my parents back home. The thing inside of me was taking more of my soul and leaving me with nothing. I enjoyed the smell of fresh blood spilling onto the ground inside of the cave. The sun was coming out and there was nothing we could do. We had lost and the demons of the Underworld could no longer feed off the souls of the wolf men. I didn't have an army anymore. My wolf men were dead and a lot of their body parts were scattered across the ground. The muddy puddles inside the cave were filled with blood. Howls and growls echoed through my ears. Most of the bats flew away and went into hiding because of the sun. I sat back in the shadows of the caves and watched the werewolves walk out feeling victorious. Goon's wolf was the last to leave out. Electricity formed around his body and the energy exploded. It caused the cave to shake and rumble like a volcano exploding. He was knocking down the caves. The heavy stones fell on top of the dead bodies of a few werewolves and wolf men, smashing them flat. Some of the bats tried to escape the gravel but were crushed. Goon's beast caused a fire over the gravel that fell. I hurriedly flew away to my home at the top of the old building. I flew through the crack of the window and turned into my human form. I sat in my chair in the middle of the room and I was beyond angry.

"Got damn it!" I yelled out. I kicked over the statue that stood next to my chair and it shattered. My bat flew inside of the window and landed on the arm of my chair. It was the bat I let drink my blood and it became connected to me. I named him Red because his eyes were the color of blood. I patted his head and it squeaked.

"We lost this time, but the next time we will win and Chancy will be mine. I will weaken that warlock, Akea, before I take her away from him," I spat.

Trade in your soul and I will grant you everything your heart desires. You will have the strength of the greatest immortals, the voice said.

You already have my soul, I replied.

Not completely; you are still holding on to your old life. Let go and come to me. It feels like you are ready, it said.

What about my family in Anubi? I asked it.

We will rule Anubi, it said. The floor opened in front of me and there was a black tornado cloud inside the floor. It reminded me of the tubs in the floor back home. A black shadow with red eyes came up from the floor and stood in front of me. It walked over to me and I was hypnotized by the force. I couldn't move; all I could do was watch it. The shadow got inside of me and I screamed. My soul was burning in hell. My body was no longer used as a puppet. I became whatever it was inside of me. The elevator door opened to the top floor and Jutu walked in.

"Osiris, I need help finding Fiti!" Jutu said and I stood up. I grabbed her by the neck and raised her off the floor.

"I'm your master and you will bow down to me in my presence. Don't you ever barge into my home again," I spat and she fell down to the floor.

"I think Fiti is dead," she said and grabbed her throat.

"Good, let her burn. She wasn't useful to me anyway and you will be, too, and soon. Bathe me, and when you are done, get my clothes and you will dress me. If you don't obey me, I will cut your head off and shove a stick inside of it. I will roast your head in the pits of hell like a campfire marshmallow. Do you understand me?" I asked. I ripped her cape off and she stood in front of me, naked. She tried to cover herself up but I smacked her hands away.

"I own you, Jutu. It was I who helped Meda create you. It was my idea. The spells and the wicked within your heart is from me. Never hide anything from me because I can see right through you. I can feel your arousal," I said.

"Seth?" she asked and backed away from me.

"A demon never reveals his name, now go. We have a lot of work to do. I want Ammon to be a warrior of the Underworld and I will not stop until I get it," I said. Jutu hurriedly rushed off to prepare my bath. I picked up Red and he squeaked.

"We are going to be very busy. This city will be painted red and I will own the souls of many humans so that my warriors in the Underworld can walk on Earth."

****

A few hours later...

I pulled up the doors to the bomb shelter that was hidden underneath an abandoned house. Jutu followed me with a candle. The smell of blood and urine filled my nostrils. I turned on the light switch and my hand got caught inside a cobb web. A big, black spider crawled on my hand and rested.

"Wake up!" I yelled and blue eyes stared at me.

"Meda captured her at a party and decided to use her. She gave her Osiris's blood. Meda thought the wolf men were no longer useful. She wanted all vampires. This was something she was working on. She was dead for two days and she just recently woke up before the battle inside of the cave happened," Jutu said. I grabbed the woman's face and stared into her eyes. They turned red then blue again. I opened up her mouth and sharp fangs pricked my finger.

"A human turned vampire is a start of many things to come," I said and unchained the woman. She fell onto the dirty floor and she was weak from hunger.

"What did you all do to me?" she asked. I kneeled down beside her and caressed her face.

"I made you immortal. A night demon, a vampire. A warrior from the Underworld and a succubus to human men. Thank me later," I said. Jutu covered her body with a cape and helped her off the floor.

"What is your name?" I asked.

"It's Sarah, Sarah Baxter," she replied.

"Not anymore," I replied.

"I can't connect with Meda. I haven't seen her since the battle," Jutu said to me.

"Meda is hiding but she can't hide for long because I own her. After we leave here, find her, and kill her. Her soul will remain in the Underworld but her body must burn. She will never walk the earth again. She betrayed me," I replied.

Arya

I was still inside a dark room. I didn't hear anyone but I felt something pulling at me. I couldn't see it but I felt it taunting me. I tried to break away but I couldn't. The door opened and the candles lit up around the room. I lifted my head and Meda was staring at me.

"Your pack destroyed all of my plans!" she screamed and threw her dagger into the wall.

"All of my hard work, destroyed! Seth is very mad at me. He is going to replace me!" she screamed.

"Please, let me go! It is all over," I said.

"No it isn't! This just made him even madder and more soul hungry!" she yelled at me.

"This has nothing to do with me," I said.

"You don't get it, do you? You belong to him now, the same way I do. We are in this together, and the sooner you realize that, the better!" she said. Meda pulled her glass globe out of her cape and hurled it into the wall. She paced back and forth, chanting something in another language.

"You can turn your life around!" I shouted at her.

"Shut up, whore! Just shut the fuck up!" she screamed at me.

"I don't want this," I cried.

"You should've kept your legs closed!" she replied. The door flew open and off the hinges. It went crashing into the wall. I heard heels clicking across the floor and I sat up. Ula walked into the room and she was with her sister, Naobi. Meda tried to strike them with lightning but Ula blocked it and sent it back, slamming it into Meda's chest. Meda fell onto the floor and gasped for air.

"Oh, thank God!" I cried.

"Don't thank the gods now. You don't believe, remember," Ula said to me.

"Not now, Ula," Naobi said. The chains around my feet and hands disappeared.

"How did you find me?" I asked.

"That necklace I gave you was like an eye for me. I would've come sooner but I wanted you to learn a lesson. I wanted you to know that the gods do exist and so does evil," Naobi said. Meda stood up and threw a dagger at Naobi. Naobi caught it with her hand and squeezed the dagger until it turned to ashes.

"My old mate's offspring. Nice to meet you and I have to tell you, you are nothing like Ammon. You actually have a heart. You really do care about Arya, but too bad you belong to the other side. What is your feud with my son, Goon?" Naobi asked her.

"You all should've killed me!" Meda shouted.

"That was your king's calling. I wanted to kill you but your brother, Baki, wanted you to live because he thought all pups were innocent. You don't know what your issue is because you are misguided. There is still something inside of you. I saw you shed a tear from the necklace I gave Arya. Demons don't cry because they don't have a soul," Naobi said.

"You don't know me, bitch!" Meda yelled at Naobi and I hid behind Ula.

"Want me to whip her ass for you? I have a hair appointment and this old-fashioned, Quinn O'Hara-dressed bitch is killing my mood," Ula said with a snake slithering across the floor. The snake wrapped around Meda's leg and Meda made it burn.

"Very cute," Meda said to Ula.

"Can we please leave?" I asked.

"Not until we get to the bottom of this," Naobi replied. She walked over toward Meda.

"Why did you turn Osiris into a vampire?" Naobi asked her.

"Seth told me that if I gave him someone to help him then I would be free of the visions I see of him. I just want to be free!" Meda said.

"It's your wish," Ula said and a snake crawled down her arm. She held the snake in her hand and it turned into a sharp arrow. She threw the arrow into Meda's neck. Meda fell down and her blood ran across the floor. Ula kneeled down beside her then snapped her neck and I gasped.

"She wanted to be free, so now she is free," Ula said. I looked at Meda's body and it turned to ashes. When I walked out of the room, I realized I was still inside of Laura's apartment.

"Does the pack know about this?" I asked Naobi.

"Yes, we defeated the wolf men hours ago. They are home waiting on your return. We are done for now because this is just the beginning," Naobi said.

****

When I arrived home, the pack was happy to see me but I knew they felt uncomfortable because of the bulge in my stomach. Kanye didn't say anything to me and he looked at me with disgust. I saw a woman who I had never seen before. She was sitting on the couch and Zaan was wrapping her hand up because she had a small wound.

"Who is she?" I asked the pack.

"That is Fiti and it's a long story," Amadi said. My mother grabbed me by the hand and pulled me out of the living room and into the hallway.

"The pack is very upset behind this although no one has mentioned it. They know you played a part in the wolf men. I love you, Arya, you know I do. Why couldn't you come to me about this? Monifa is supposed to be like your little sister. You have to look out for her the same way you do for Baneet and Chancy. Monifa came back into the house after the battle and we all thought she was hurt because she was attacked by a witch. But when she came home, her body temperature was very hot and she was in pain from cramping. Her uterus is preparing her for an immortal pregnancy. I'm telling you because even though you mated with Kanye, he is still going to mate with his soulmate. But I'm here for you all the way even though I'm upset that you are carrying a demon pup. If you feel like you don't have anyone, just remember you will always have me," she said. She kissed my cheek and walked away. Baneet stepped out into the hallway. She placed her hand over my stomach.

"Wow, it really does go fast. I want to talk to you about the other night. I'm sorry for saying all of those things to you," she said and I squeezed her hand.

"It's no big deal. I'm just glad to be back home," I said. I looked into the living room and we watched Zaan flirt with Fiti.

"She's beautiful but she doesn't compare to you," I said after I noticed the scowl on Baneet's face.

"She's a witch from Anubi. She needs Goon and Naobi's help to get her back there. I don't know why she has to be here," Baneet spat. Elle came down the hallway and he was with someone. It was a male wolf from another pack.

"What is Geo doing inside our house? What if Zaan finds out he is the wolf you were cheating on him with?" I said.

"Geo was hurt in the fight and Kanye's dumb ass brought him here so that Elle and Amadi could dress up his wound. Too bad he is not a fast healer like us," Baneet said. Geo was the alpha of another pack. He limped passed Baneet and winked at her.

"Ay, are you good? Do you need anything before you leave?" Zaan asked Geo when he walked out of the living room.

"No, I'm fine. I've got to get home to my sister and brothers. They don't know where I'm at," he replied and looked at Baneet while Zaan gave him a handshake. Geo was handsome in a boyish type of way. His skin was the color of a Hershey's bar and he was tall. He stood at about six-foot-four and had the cutest set of dimples with slanted eyes and a strong jawline. He was the youngest alpha in the area with a pack because his parents were killed.

"Thanks a lot. Too bad after today, we will be banned from each other's territory," Zaan said and Geo chuckled.

"Not banned from everything," Geo said and limped to the front door. He winked at Baneet again before he left out of the house. Zaan looked at Baneet and his eyes were trying to read her.

"I will be in your room later so we can finish talking," Baneet said and rushed off. I headed upstairs and Taj was coming out of a guest room. He wore sweatpants and a black wife beater. I rolled my eyes at him and he chuckled.

"If I didn't know any better, I would assume that you hate me," he said.

"I think you are annoying. The fight is over and we thank you for your help, but why are you still here?" I asked.

"Maybe I want to hang around to make your day brighter," he said.

"I'm carrying a pup," I replied.

"That doesn't belong to you or Kanye," he said. I growled at him and slapped his face. Three long scratches appeared on his cheek. He looked at me and smirked while his wound closed then whispered in my ear.

"Usually the dogs chase the cats but I'm willing to chase after you, Arya," Taj said.

"We are natural born enemies. I hate cats," I spat and he laughed.

"Then we can leave our beasts at home. What if I like you this way? As the woman that is standing in front of me? I can tame my tiger and he is a good boy when I do," he said and his voice sent chills up my spine.

"Tigers are circus cats. I'm sure they can be tamed by their owners," I said.

"And wolves are big house dogs that wag their tails when they see a bone. Well, I have a bone for you and it gives mind-blowing orgasms. I will make your little puppy beg for mercy. I will turn that pussy into a pussycat. When you are done fighting it, you can find me across town in my loft," he said and walked away from me.

****

It's only a matter of time before you will join me, the voice said. It was the same voice I heard when I mated with Kanye.

Who are you? I asked.

You gave your body to me and pretty soon my master will release my soul and I will walk on Earth. You will see me soon and I will be there to take what belongs to me, it said. I opened my eyes and I was still in the bath tub in my bedroom bathroom. I hurriedly crawled out and dried off. I slid my arms into my robe and I felt my pup move. Whatever it was that was haunting me wanted my pup. I walked out of the bathroom and headed toward my bed. Someone knocked on my door.

"Come in!" I called out. Kanye walked into my room and my heart dropped to my stomach. He looked at my stomach and growled. I closed my robe tighter to hide it.

"I'm sorry, Kanye. I really am," I said and he crossed his arms. He was driving me crazy and I felt that desire for him again.

"Me, too," he said.

"How is Monifa feeling? I heard she was injured badly," I said. I honestly didn't care how she felt because she had no rights to Kanye. I believed in the gods but I still didn't believe that he was made for Monifa. She didn't deserve him because she was also a witch. There wasn't any doubt in my mind that she cursed him. Witches belonged to their own kind.

"She's getting her strength back but I came in here to talk to you about the pup you are carrying," he said.

"What about it?" I asked.

"I don't want a muthafuckin' thing to do with it. That thing is not my pup. I'm glad you are safe but I'm pissed you even showed your face. I blame all of this on you. Laura was Meda the whole time? Those wolf men were your ideas? You should leave," he said.

"This is my pack, too!" I yelled at him.

"If you don't leave by morning, I will tear your damn neck away from your head. I will rip you to shreds and bury you in the backyard. Oh, yeah, it's the dog in me," he growled.

"I will leave," I said. He left out of the room, slamming my door shut and it flew off the hinges. I grabbed my things and started packing suitcases. Meda was right, I didn't belong to my pack. I waited until everyone in the house was asleep before I made my way out the door.

After I put my things inside my car, I drove off. I looked back at the mansion behind me when I drove up to the gate and a tear fell from my eye. I was going to be on my own. Just me and my pup. I was going to miss the pack but I was going to miss my mother, Anik, even more.

Akea

I was finally outside of Kanye. I knew the key to our connection—our energy at its greatest point joined, and it fell apart after our energy was weakened. I disappeared out of his body seconds later after we got home from the battle because Kanye's beast was exhausted. His energy could no longer hold me inside of him. The birds were chirping when I woke up that morning. I climbed out of bed and stretched. Our pack was safe at the moment but Osiris was still alive and our father was going to Anubi with Naobi. I walked into my bathroom and Chancy was throwing up in the toilet. Her canines hung over her bottom lip and her nails dug into the toilet bowl. Her hair was stuck to her face and her body was hot and clammy.

I kneeled down beside her and rubbed her back. I wanted to tell Dayo about me and his daughter but I couldn't find the right time. Chancy was sneaking into my room when everyone was asleep and I was afraid that she was going to get caught. I didn't want nobody to find out that way. The thing with Arya pushed Dayo away from the pack. He was angry that she was carrying a demon pup, so he stayed out in the woods. When she came home, he didn't come into the house because he couldn't see her that way.

"What is the matter with you?" I asked Chancy and wrapped my arm around her. I felt something inside of her stomach and I placed my hand over it. I felt an extra heartbeat and I pulled away from her.

"I think that deer I ate was sick or something," she said and fell into me. I grabbed the rag on the sink and wiped her forehead off.

"We are in deep shit," I said.

"Why?" she asked.

"You are pregnant," I said. The vision I had of Osiris turning Chancy while carrying my seed played into my head again. I thought it was going to go away because we won the battle but that was not the case. Everything that happened was leading up to that moment, and if my vision was true, Osiris was possessed by the king of the Underworld.

Monifa

I woke up to Kanye kissing on my lips and I pushed him off the bed.

"You definitely feel better now," he said and laid on top of me.

"I'm still cramping, now get off of me," I spat. I climbed out of the bed and opened up the window in his bedroom. His naked body stood behind me and he wrapped his arms around me. His teeth sank into my neck and his tongue gently licked my sensitive spot.

"Our mating moon is in a few days," he whispered in my ear.

"I know," I said sadly.

"I'm still your mate, Monifa. There is nothing you can do about that. I will never intentionally hurt you. We have our own destiny together. You will help out with me and Akea's jewelry store. We will have pups and we can pass the store down to them when they get older. I saw the vision last night while I was asleep. I love you," he said. I turned around and faced him.

"I just feel like a part of me is gone. She is connected to you because she is carrying your pup. I can't control how I feel because of how I feel about you. It pains me deeply that she has a piece of you," I said.

"You are connected to me and I am to you. We are for eternity no matter what. I know what you need," he said and grabbed his basketball shorts. He slid his feet into his Nike house shoes. He grabbed his hoodie off a chair and zipped it up.

"All you need is some cow meat with a glass of warm milk with honey," he said and kissed my lips. I noticed a change in him. He could sense what I craved without me telling him or him reading my thoughts. It was the connection that was between us.

"Where are you going to get cow meat?" I asked.

"There's a farm a few miles away. I'm going to let the cow loose then hunt it," he replied. He leaped out of his window and landed on his feet. He took off running toward the woods. I wondered if what I did was wicked. While Kanye was asleep the night before, I went into Arya's room as him. While I was Kanye, I could see the love she had for him. I heard her thoughts and I felt the desire she craved. She still wanted him to enter her body. She felt no sympathy for me when she asked if I was okay from the battle.

Sorry Arya but you weren't playing fair and neither am I, I thought.

Beasts: A Mate's War

Coming Soon...

Made in the USA
Columbia, SC
29 August 2024

41286000R00185